Model
Soldier

Red Hot & Blue

SPECIAL BONUS EDITION
includes BB DALTON

Cat Johnson

New York Times & USA Today Bestselling Author

First Edition 2008
Reprint 2018

ISBN-13: 978-1983679452
ISBN-10: 1983679453

RED HOT & BLUE

Red Blooded
Smalltown Heat
A Few Good Men
BB Dalton
Model Soldier
A Prince Among Men
True Blue

What readers are saying about
MODEL SOLDIER

"heart-pounding adventure on the edge of the war torn
Middle East" ~ Sizzling Hot Book Reviews

"Fun and intense and sweet and so much more" ~Night Owl
Book Reviews

"Model Soldier isn't anyone's fairy tale, but has the real life
bumps and bruises that come with falling in love, combined
with the realities of life and war. A great story and
continuation of a series that highlight the men in uniform we
all love." ~Joyfully Reviewed

CHAPTER ONE

"Out of every one hundred men, ten shouldn't even be there, eighty are just targets, nine are the real fighters, and we are lucky to have them, for they make the battle. Ah, but the one. One is a warrior and he will bring the others back."
Heraclitus, 500 B.C.

Late 2007

Army Staff Sergeant David *Hawk* Hawkins kneeled and surveyed the barren wasteland of the icy terrain ahead.

Gusts of brisk winter air howled across the desolation. The frigid area was vacant of all life save his squad.

Exhaling, Hawk watched his breath freeze before him in mid-air.

With the raise of a gloved hand, he signaled his men. The silent wraiths emerged from the ground, cloaked in the arctic mist. The only sign of their corporeal selves was the barely discernible crunch of snow beneath boots.

Upon his signal, Hawk's squad stealthily approached their final destination on the side of the mountain.

He was beginning to feel as though his many sins had come to bear and his sentence was this God-forsaken place. This mountain had become his personal Hell.

Hawk decided to err on the side of caution and signaled for a short halt as he considered the juggernaut before them.

Through frozen lips, he whispered as softly as a lover's caress into his radio, "Bravo, take overwatch. Alpha, move out."

As they'd traveled this path to Hell over the past few hours—hours that seemed more like days—Hawk had divided his squad into two teams. Two entities separate yet bound together, one always supporting the other, providing security.

He'd chosen his two best men to lead the teams, soldiers he would soon have to trust, not only with his own life, but also with the lives of them all.

Without a word, the two groups responded to his order by moving quickly and surely into position.

The overwatch team opened fire into the rocks above. The belch of gunfire erupted and broke through the icy stillness. Tracers flew through the icy air like mad yellow jackets on a late autumn day.

Hawk hit the rocky ground hard, knowing his body would pay later. But right now, he couldn't feel a thing, not while adrenaline surged through his veins as enemy fire struck the snow-covered rocks protecting him.

A too-familiar pop sounded.

With no time for the radio, he shouted, "RPG! Take cover!"

The rocket propelled grenade cut a trail through the air, exploding nearby and showering him with debris as he lay behind cover.

While his men returned that less-than-friendly greeting with their own volley, he engaged the selector lever on his rifle with his thumb as his forefinger slipped onto the trigger.

The scene seemed to move frame by frame to Hawk's eye as his brain and body, both on autopilot, processed and reacted to the situation.

Visually, Hawk traced the path the RPG had taken back to its owner whose fate was decided the moment he began to rise from cover before Hawk's sights.

Hawk squeezed the trigger.

Following the quick burst from his barrel, Hawk barely took the time to watch the man fall before he yelled, "Bravo team, maintain supportive fire."

With Bravo suppressing the enemy above, Hawk sprung from the ground and sprinted to join Alpha team.

Diving behind protective cover, he knew he had to choose the next course wisely.

"Alpha team, follow me." Hawk issued the order as he began to maneuver far right in an attempt to flank his opposition.

Using a partially covered route as the supportive fire kept the enemy pinned in place, he moved quickly.

"Shit." Hawk hissed as his boot slipped on the treacherous footing.

Moving too rapidly in this terrain could mean a fall from what was in all probability a deadly height, while moving too slowly could give the enemy the advantage and mean his squad's demise.

After taking a calming breath that would hopefully reach down to steady his feet, Hawk ran. A few enemy shots peppered the path around him. There was no choice but to accept the risk and drive forward if he wanted to win this.

Through his headset, Hawk heard the good news that Bravo team had scratched two and continued to suppress the remaining enemy element. Two less opposition to worry about as Alpha team got into place to assault from the right.

Hawk waited until the last possible moment before he ordered, "B team. We're in position. Lift and shift fire."

And please try and not hit us. He added a silent prayer to whatever godly force aided soldiers in battle that none of his men would fall to fratricide.

He saw the enemy scramble. Having been pinned down, they failed to see Hawk's approach until too late. As they attempted to swing their weapons to ward off the surprise attack to their right flank, they fell one by one.

To their credit, or perhaps as a testament to their stupidity, none tried to surrender, but instead fought to the bitter end.

After a quick survey to ensure his own men were still standing, a small smile crossed his ice-cold lips as he allowed himself barely a breath to enjoy the victory.

Many a dead man had learned too late not to celebrate prematurely. There was still much to do. "Bravo, establish security. Alpha, search the area."

His men, who up until this moment had been silent and efficient, transformed into jubilant boys, filling the air with whoops and chatter as soon as they had completed the quick job of checking the downed opposing team and clearing the training weapons from them.

Shaking his head at their behavior, he didn't bother to correct them.

This had been a training exercise, not an actual mission, so he supposed he could cut them some slack. They had been swift and the work was already done.

"Team One to Base. This is Hawk. Over." Hawk called in to base to report the situation and do a bit of bragging of his own.

"Go ahead, Hawk. Over."

"The enemy has been eliminated. Awaiting further orders. Over."

"Return to base for debriefing. Over," the disembodied voice told him.

"Copy that. Over and out." Hawk sighed and looked at the crimson-spotted snow surrounding him.

He'd led his team to victory, but in what amounted to a glorified game of paintball.

His only hope, when the time came months in the future, was to bring all his men back from Afghanistan to their loved ones, alive and unscathed.

Well, perhaps that wasn't his only wish. He wouldn't mind something warm in his belly right now—coffee, food or whisky, any of the three would suffice. Hell, he wasn't picky.

While he was wishing, he hoped the journey back down to base would be easier than the one here. There was no way it could be any worse.

As he and the team negotiated the frigid path to base, Hawk soon realized he couldn't have been more wrong.

"Fuck." Hawk lowered his head against the driving wind. He couldn't help thinking his protective facemask wasn't doing so great a job of protecting him at the moment.

"Sergeant?" Ryan Pettit questioned his comment. Pettit, Hawk's second in command and the man who'd led Alpha team that day, squinted against the sudden snow squall that blew tiny ice daggers into all their eyes.

"Nothing, Pettit. It's just I think I cursed us. I'd hoped the trip back down would be easy. This is what I get for that." Hawk shook his head at his foolishness.

His Alpha-team leader laughed. "Well, you know what they say. Put your hopes in one hand and shit in the other hand and see which one fills up fastest."

Hawk laughed at that jest.

Wally, aka Trent Wallace, his Bravo-team leader, emerged out of the blizzard from somewhere next to Pettit. He looked about as miserable as Hawk felt.

Visibility was limited pretty much to the distance of his hand in front of his face. Thank God, they'd finished off the enemy before this shit hit.

"I thought it was wishes, not hopes. Put your wishes in one hand and shit in the other." Wally sounded like his mouth was frozen. They were all talking a little funny at the moment. Impending frostbite does that to a person.

"Hopes, wishes, same damn thing." Looking grim, Pettit swiped at his face with one gloved hand, knocking away the snow that had built up on his eyelashes and brows.

"Yeah. Pretty much." Hawk had to agree. Hopes, wishes, both were useless.

Starting to look like the abominable snowman himself, Hawk began feeling uncharacteristically superstitious, probably due to hypothermia and hunger. Then and there, he swore to himself he'd remember in the future not to do either, wishing or hoping. Not if this kind of torture was the result.

Thanks to the sudden storm, the journey down the mountain took them twice as long as the trip up. The only solace being that they walked away victorious and without any losses.

When they finally arrived at base, Hawk gladly sent his men back to their temporary lodging to eat and get warm.

Meanwhile, he sat and waited, not so gladly, to be debriefed by the commanding training officer in charge of this shindig.

The man was taking his sweet damn time too, long enough that Hawk had the opportunity to lean his head back against the wall in the warm office, close his eyes and review the day, his life, his future . . .

This much reflection was definitely evidence that he was deliriously tired. As his thoughts drifted aimlessly, he couldn't help but wonder where the hell the time had gone.

It seemed as if he'd just gotten back to Germany from his third deployment in Iraq. Yet here he was, in the field once more. In the freaking Alps no less, for a mission-readiness exercise. But he'd do whatever it took, even freezing his ass off in the Alps, to prepare his new unit before they headed out again, this time for Afghanistan. The Kabul Province, to be exact.

He'd thought Iraq had been bad, but from what he'd heard, Afghanistan made Iraq look like the frigging French Riviera. Awaiting them in the far mountainous outskirts of the city of Kabul would be a few makeshift shacks for living areas, a generator or two and a small cooking area. That was the extent of what he'd been told they could expect to find in the way of comfort.

Supplies would have to be flown in by chopper to reach them. He'd heard there had been improvements and that more may be done before he arrived. One could only hope.

Not that it mattered how sparse or unimproved conditions were, they would still complete their assigned mission.

He and his men had been so busy the past few months, using their combined experience from their tours in the sandbox to help train the guys in other units at the garrison in Hohenfels, they'd pretty much gotten the shaft for time to train themselves for this new deployment. At least until today, when this last-minute exercise in the Alps had been thrown at them.

Hawk hoped they all wouldn't pay the price for lack of preparedness once they hit Afghanistan. There, the platoon would be doing dismounted ops the majority of the time, far from assistance and farther from home.

But he wasn't in Afghanistan yet. Instead, he sat here at base camp on the mountain infamous for breaking people, trying to recover from one of the hardest damn training exercises he'd ever been through.

In fact, he'd hardly thought about his upcoming deployment in hours since the mock "enemy" force he'd faced today demanded every last scrap of his attention.

The current situation made last week's two days of training and live-fire exercises in the field back at his home base at Hohenfels look like a walk in the park, even with the freezing temperatures and five inches of snow on the ground.

Compared to the conditions here, that workout had been nothing.

The German Army prepared on the very same rocky terrain where Hawk had trained today. Many areas reportedly had up to four feet of snow. Hawk could only think that the Army sent them here because these were the same conditions they could expect to find in the mountains separating Afghanistan and Pakistan. The same region where Osama bin Laden's boys still maintained a stronghold in spite of all the good guys' efforts.

Today, Hawk's unit had faced some supposedly elite Special Operations team sent in by Central Command to play the part of the bad guys to ready them for Afghanistan.

CentCom's handpicked golden boys were good, but not good enough.

Hawk's squad, ten soldiers plus himself, had grown to be one hell of a force. Good enough to whip this Task Force

Zeta's ass up and down the side of that God-forsaken mountain.

The sound of a door opening broke into Hawk's thoughts. His eyes flew open in time to see the black-clad, gray-haired training commander enter the room.

Standing, Hawk took the commander's offered hand and shook it while trying to ignore how much effort it took to even raise his arm from his side.

"Sergeant Hawkins. You did well up there today." Commander Miller, the man in charge of this show, greeted him.

They did well? They'd done fucking great, was more like it. But instead of voicing that opinion, Hawk inclined his head and accepted the compliment.

"I can't take credit for the complete molding of them, sir. I have one strong team leader and the other is decent. He's a bit rough around the edges, but I'm working to fix that. Together, the team leaders and I have trained the rest of the Joes."

He'd gotten them to where he needed them to be, acting together, their movements fluid. They were efficient killers when needed. Capable of identifying the enemy amongst a crowd and engaging only those who were combatants. Following his orders without question or complaint and taking down the bad guys without hesitation or regret.

Commander Miller smiled and elbowed the man who had followed him into the room. "Damn. I guess I shouldn't have told you guys to go easy on them. I would have loved to see what they could really do. What do you think, Dalton?"

"The guys would have loved to play full out. I thought Bull would lose his mind having to hold back like that. Maybe next time." The Task Force Zeta Operative Hawk recognized as leading the opposing team in today's exercise shrugged casually.

Hawk swung his gaze from this Dalton guy to the commander. "Excuse me?"

"Yes, Sergeant?" Miller raised a brow.

Shaking his head in disbelief, Hawk practically sputtered with anger. "You had your team hold back?"

"Nothing to worry about, soldier. I would never expect your squad to compete against Zeta when they play full out. Go and get some rest. And again, good job up there today." Miller slapped Hawk on the shoulder then turned to go.

Anger-fueled and breaking all protocol, Hawk grabbed Miller's arm. "Run the exercise again." Then he added a quick, "Sir," and then a, "please."

Although a little sojourn in the brig for insubordination would provide him some much needed rest, Hawk figured it was probably best to avoid it if possible.

Miller shook his head. "You won, son. There's no need."

The commander's eyes lowered briefly to Hawk's hand, still on him. Hawk dropped his hold immediately, but not the subject.

"There's no victory for me if your team didn't go full out. Do you think the insurgents in Afghanistan will be holding back when they face my men?" Hawk stifled anything else he might have wanted to say before he did end up in the brig.

An amused look crossed Miller's face as his gaze moved from Hawk to his team leader for this exercise.

"Dalton?" Miller questioned the man with one word.

"He does have a point there, commander. And our guys would really enjoy being able to kick some ass unrestrained." A cocky grin crossed pretty-boy Dalton's face, just begging to be knocked off with the help of Hawk's fist.

"All right. I'll call Gordon back at the rear to confirm nothing's come up that requires the team's immediate attention. But barring that, you get your wish, soldier. I'll see you and your squad here at zero-four-thirty."

Hawk's men were not going to be happy when he informed them they'd be traipsing around outside in God only knew how much fresh powder at zero-dark-thirty instead of dreaming in their racks. All because of him and his damn pride. Hawk mouthed a silent curse.

Dalton noticed and laughed. "You walked right into that

one, Sergeant Hawkins."

Yeah, he'd really like to slug this guy right in his smug face all right. But for now, he had to go break the news to his men that they were not only spending one more night and day on this mountain, but they wouldn't be doing a hell of a lot of sleeping either.

The commander's words echoed in his head. *"You get your wish, soldier."*

Hawk's final thought as a smiling Dalton closed the door of the office behind him was that he really had to remember to stop wishing.

CHAPTER TWO

The problem with mothers was this—you had to love them, even when you didn't like them very much.

Annoyed, Emily Price considered this as she felt her hand go numb from her tight grip on the phone receiver.

Meanwhile, her mother continued to regale her with tales of exactly how wonderful Emily's flawless sister Lily was for taking her shopping the other day, which Emily never did.

Perhaps that was because Lily and their mother both lived in Chicago, while Emily lived and worked, very hard she might add, in New York.

She didn't bother bringing up that small yet pertinent fact. It would only restart another familiar ritual battle, that being why didn't Emily move back home or at the very least visit more often?

For what? So she could feel inadequate next to her sister? Perfect Lily, whose hair had always been blonder than Emily's, whose grades had always been higher, whose boyfriends had always been nicer . . .

"Emily Rose. I can tell you're not listening to me."

Uh, oh. Had she forgotten to mindlessly respond at what her mother felt was the appropriate time during her diatribe?

"Are you playing on that computer of yours again while I'm trying to talk to you?" The accusation in her mother's tone came loud and clear through the receiver held in Emily's death grip.

Playing. Yeah, because working for the busiest woman on the face of the earth, or at least on Madison Avenue, was all fun and games.

Resorting to base instinct as she held onto her temper and her sanity by the tips of her fingernails, Emily knew the time had come for fight or flight. She had to choose one and soon, because she wasn't going to make it on this phone call one minute more without blowing up.

"I'm sorry, Mom. My boss really needs me. I've got to go. Call you back soon. Love you. Bye."

She managed to stifle the long, loud, pent-up groan waiting in her throat until after she'd slammed the receiver down into the cradle, using a bit more force than necessary to disconnect the call.

Emily took one more glance at the display to make sure she really had totally and completely hung up before letting her head drop to the desk.

After a bit, the slow, steady thudding of Emily's head banging against the desktop ceased, leaving only the soft sound of her boss's snicker.

"How come in your fibs I always have to be the bad boss who makes you hang up on your mother? I think I'm insulted. I'm a nice person. I would never do that for real."

"Oh, shut up." Emily groaned, forehead still pressed against the cool, smooth wooden surface. "You're an only child, Katie. You can't possibly understand what I go through with my mother and sister."

"Now, now. I'm dating a man with eight siblings, so I've gotten quite an education from BB in this area."

BB Dalton, only the hottest as well as nicest man on earth, was Katie's boyfriend. Another reason to hate her besides her lack of siblings. She had the perfect man in her life.

Brushing the hair out of her face, Emily glanced past tousled blonde bangs and noticed her boss's face had turned deathly white.

Sitting straight, she was about to ask what was wrong when Katie jumped from her chair. Her boss pressed one hand over her mouth and ran from the room.

Frowning and concerned, Emily leapt to follow her. "Katie?"

"I'll be fine." The muffled response was all Emily heard before the restroom door slammed shut.

She'd have to wait until Katie emerged to interrogate her further about the sudden departure. Emily perched on the edge of Katie's desk to wait when a distinct scent caught her attention.

Searching for the source, Emily discovered something very strange sitting innocently amid her boss's cluttered mess. Suddenly, it all started to make sense.

She was still leaning on Katie's desk holding the suspicious object in question when the ailing woman finally returned.

"What is this?" Emily held up her evidence. She'd probably spoken sterner than she should to a woman who was obviously suffering.

Katie's face paled once again. "Um, that's my coffee mug."

"Yes, it is your coffee mug." Emily nodded. "And you love coffee. You can't live without coffee. You grind your own beans for God's sake. So why, oh why, is there tea in your coffee mug? Caffeine-free herbal tea, no less."

To prove her point, Emily sniffed the minty aroma, already suspecting she knew the answer.

Striding forward but still visibly woozy, Katie grabbed the mug from Emily's hands. "A person can try something new once in a while. Can't she?"

Katie sat heavily in the desk chair, slumping rather than displaying her usual perfect posture that went along with the perfect rest of her.

Apparently sensing she was still under Emily's scrutiny, Katie avoided eye contact, studiously shuffling a few papers on her crowded desk. "Where is that file for the Army ad campaign? You know, we still need to find a model for that."

"Stop trying to change the subject." Emily scowled at the obvious diversionary tactic.

Still not looking up, Katie shook her head. "Jeez. An inquisition over a little cup of mint tea."

With a new idea, Emily made her way to the small kitchenette in the office. There they stored the necessities in case they had to throw together a quick show of hospitality for some big client or talent on the spur of the moment. The fridge was always stocked with bottled water, both bubbly and flat, an assortment of fruit and cheeses, champagne and chardonnay.

What Emily needed was in the cabinet. She reached past the bottles of red wine on the lower shelf to grab a box of unopened, plain water crackers from above.

After dropping the box on the desk, Emily crossed her arms and stood over Katie. "Eat some. It will help. My sister couldn't get enough of those when she was pregnant."

Katie's gaze shot up and a guilty expression marred her face. "How'd you know?"

"Hmm. I don't know. Turning green and running for the bathroom. No more caffeine for the coffee junky . . ." Emily raised a brow and ticked off the proof on her fingers. She paused and waited for Katie's imminent confession.

"I'm so sorry I didn't tell you. I haven't told anyone yet except BB."

"Why? You know you can trust me. You can tell me anything and I'd take it to the grave. That's what assistants and friends are for."

Tears glistened in Katie's eyes. "I know." She paused and glanced around the office until Emily handed her a tissue from the box on the corner of the desk behind her. "Thank you. And it's not that I don't trust you. It's my body I don't trust. Em, I'm forty. I'm too old to be pregnant with my first child."

"No, you're not. How old was BB's mom when she had him?"

"That doesn't count. He was her ninth."

"That doesn't matter. And besides, things are different nowadays. Women are having babies into their fifties. Modern medicine has all these tests and stuff. It's perfectly safe."

Katie laughed tearfully. "This coming from a girl in her twenties with nice young eggs and a good firm uterus." Emily rolled her eyes as Katie continued, "I'm just so afraid. BB doesn't want to show me how excited he is because he knows how worried I am, but I know he's totally in love with the idea of being a dad. Em, what if I miscarry?"

"BB is totally in love with you, and he will continue to be no matter what happens."

"I know that, when I can think straight. I'm just so emotional and irrational lately." Wiping her eyes, Katie looked up. Her gaze met Emily's. "I'm sorry to lay this all on you."

"Don't you dare apologize. I'm here for you. You know that. I'm sorry you're feeling so badly. Where's BB right now? I'll cover work for you if you want to fly down to the base and visit him. That might make you feel better."

Being in the arms of a hottie like BB would surely make Emily feel better.

Katie laughed at that. "No, no need for you to cover for me. He's in the Alps. That flight is a bit too long for me at the moment. There wouldn't be enough barf bags on the plane for a trip as far as Germany."

Emily bit her lip. "Were you supposed to tell me that he's in Germany? Isn't where he goes top secret?"

BB was some sort of super-secret Special Operative.

"If it was classified he wouldn't have been able to tell me, so I couldn't have told you, now could I?" Katie raised a brow.

That sounded reasonable enough, but working with the military on their marketing had been a lesson in rules, both rational and not. "Mmm. I guess so. Can I ask one more thing?"

"Sure." Katie tried to break into the cracker box as she

began to pale again.

After watching her struggle with the cellophane wrapping, Emily grabbed the box out of her hands, tore it open and handed it back. "Are there terrorists hiding in the Alps now too?"

Katie chewed and swallowed a cracker and then shook her head. "Not that I know of, but I suppose anything is possible nowadays. He said it's just a training exercise. Commander Miller brought BB's task force in to help train some Army guys. No big deal, he said. Nothing to worry about . . ." Katie's voice trailed off.

Long-distance relationships were tough. This one with BB was even more so given his occupation. Emily knew Katie did worry, each and every time her boyfriend and his mysterious task-force buddies disappeared for an undetermined amount of time to parts unknown.

With a baby added to the mix that worry and the frequent separations would only be worse for Katie.

That raised the next question that had yet to be answered. "What are you two going to do, you know, about getting married? I mean it's totally cool if you have a baby and don't get married. People do that all the time."

Katie laughed. "Don't worry. BB asks me to marry him every day. Sometimes twice a day."

"And you haven't said yes yet?" What was wrong with this woman?

"I finally did a few days ago." Katie smiled weakly. "He wore me down. Either that, or it was the hormones talking."

Emily clapped her hands together. She didn't care what had caused it, as long as it happened. "Yay! A wedding to plan. I love weddings."

"Hang on just a minute. I told him I'll only marry him if I make it past my third month without . . . you know."

"How far along are you now?"

Katie wasn't showing at all. Although now that Emily thought about it, did Katie's boobs seem to be straining the buttons on her shirt a bit?

"Eight weeks, closer to nine actually if the doctor calculated correctly. Only two months in and already I can barely ride in a car without getting carsick and my breasts hurt so badly they feel like they are about to explode."

Emily nodded in sympathy. "Yeah, my sister said that too. It doesn't last the whole time. Don't worry. But hey, you're more than two thirds of the way to that three-month marker. Besides, I have a good feeling about this. You wouldn't be having all these symptoms if that baby wasn't planted in there nice and firmly, right?"

Katie laughed. "I guess so."

"So we need to start planning, just in case. The good wedding places book up a year in advance or more—"

"No. No big plans. If this wedding happens, it will be small."

Emily let out a snort. "He has eight brothers and sisters. Exactly how small can it be?"

Katie groaned and slumped lower in her chair. For a high-powered New York marketing executive, her boss could sure be an introvert. "I know. That's why I told him I want to elope."

"Elope?" Emily's hopes fell.

"Relax. You'll be there, even if we end up at a drive-thru in Vegas married by an Elvis impersonator. I promise."

Well, that was something at least.

"Okay. Thanks." That she'd get to be there for the ceremony softened the disappointment a bit, but not enough. Emily thought longingly about all the missed opportunities to visit bridal shops and watch Katie try on long white, or perhaps off-white, dresses.

"Don't look so dejected, Em. You'll get your chance one day, and then you can plan as big a wedding as you want for yourself. I'll even help you."

"Yeah, sure, because the men are just knocking down the door to marry me." Emily rolled her eyes.

Katie shook her head. "I've never seen such a bright, attractive, kind-hearted woman spend so many Saturday nights without a date."

"Hey, that used to be my complaint about you," Emily reminded.

"Yes, it was, but now you don't have to worry about me or my love life anymore. I not only got myself a boyfriend, I also got knocked up. So go out and find yourself your perfect guy."

"Are any of BB's brothers single?" Good looks were genetic. The Dalton brothers would have to be at least as hot as BB.

"No, sorry. He's the youngest. The rest are all married off already."

Hmm, that was disappointing. "Any of his military guy friends single?"

"No military guys for you." There was a warning in Katie's voice.

Emily frowned. "Why do you say it like that?"

"Because one of us dating a Special Operative is enough stress. Believe me." Katie crossed her arms over her chest. "Go find your own guy. A nice civilian businessman or maybe a construction worker. The city is full of them both."

Maybe she didn't want a boring normal guy.

"Some help you are." Feeling spiteful, Emily went to pour herself a nice, big steaming cup of caffeinated coffee.

As payback she intended to drink it right in front of Katie. That would punish her boss for hogging the hot military men for herself.

CHAPTER THREE

What the hell? Hawk frowned and counted the opposing team gathered at the rally point one more time.

"Problem?" There was that smug, pretty-boy smile again that Hawk had come to hate on Dalton's face.

Yeah, there was a frigging problem.

"Your team seems to have grown overnight." Hawk sounded much more casual than he felt about that fact.

He was sure his ten guys plus himself could take them, but that was still no reason to be happy Zeta was basically cheating by changing the rules mid-way into the game.

Pretty Boy Dalton nodded. "Ah. That. Yeah, when you told the commander you wanted Zeta to go all out, he called the rear and ordered the rest of the team over."

That put Zeta at a whopping seven men, not counting the commander who made eight. Two more than Hawk's men had faced during the prior day's exercise.

On top of the extra manpower, they also had brought in some sophisticated computer shit. One of the new arrivals seemed to know how to use it as his fingers flew over the keys of not one but three laptops.

Noticing where Hawk's gaze rested, Dalton grinned. "Zeta wouldn't be Zeta without Matt Coleman the computer god and all his equipment."

Extra guys and state-of-the-art equipment. Fucking

cheaters. All Hawk and his squad had access to was what amounted to basic walkie-talkies, and they were happy when they worked correctly.

Hawk let out a sigh. He noticed Dalton seemed to be waiting for a response to what really hadn't been a question, but more of a boast that CentCom gave SpecOps better toys than Hawk's squad got.

Cocking his head, Hawk mustered a grin equal to Dalton's. "If your team thinks they need all that shit to beat us, then you go ahead and feel free to use it. My guys, however, don't need anything more than what we had yesterday to beat you. Just our wits and our skill."

Dalton broke into an all-out laugh. "I admire your confidence, Hawkins, but—"

Hawk watched as Dalton broke off mid-sentence and seemed to be hearing voices in his head. Pretty Boy's smile disappeared and the concentration became evident by the expression on his face.

When Dalton said softly, "BB here. Roger that," Hawk was sure of it. Pretty Boy was either crazy as a loon or actually talking to someone in his head.

"As I was saying, Hawkins, I admire your confidence, but there's no way your squad can beat Zeta."

When Dalton continued with his insults as if nothing out of the ordinary had just happened, Hawk really got pissed.

"What the hell was that all about?" Hawk pointed a finger at Dalton's ear to indicate the previous more than strange occurrence.

Although Hawk could see damn well that it was all an act, Dalton pondered the ceiling for a moment as he seemed to consider his answer carefully. Dalton was clearly fucking with him, playing mind games.

"Well, it's top secret, but I figure I can tell you since you're going to need all the help you can get today." Dalton looked extra cocky and tapped a finger to his right ear. "Cochlear communications implants. Whole team has them."

Fuck.

Hawk had heard rumors about SpecOps having communications devices actually surgically implanted in their frigging ears, but he'd thought it was bullshit. Maybe it was all still bullshit and Dalton was just messing with him.

But no, as Hawk glanced around the room he noticed more than one team member get the same glazed look and then respond to no one, including the damn training commander, Miller.

One look at their supposed computer god told Hawk that Coleman was the puppet master, testing his toys, one by one. No wonder they'd needed him flown in for today.

"You still up for this?" Dalton donned a gleeful smile, his perfect teeth nearly blinding Hawk with their whiteness.

Hawk had never been one to back down from a challenge, no matter what the odds. "Hell yeah, I'm still up for this. You boys can talk to each other in your heads all you want, but you pampered SuperOps still won't be able to hold up against battle-toughened soldiers trained with real-world mission experience."

He watched as Dalton rose nicely to that challenge.

"Oh really? Would you like to make this a bit more interesting? A little wager perhaps?" Pretty Boy raised a brow.

Sure, Dalton would want to make a bet since he probably took home three times what Hawk did in military pay in addition to what was probably a huge basic allowance for housing, while Hawk made do with living in the bachelor barracks.

Hawk shook his head and swallowed his pride. "I'm not much into betting for money, Dalton."

Pretty Boy nodded. "Fine. Not for money then. Something else."

Hawk frowned. "Like what?"

The other man shrugged and then, as if a bulb had been turned on in his tiny brain, Dalton's face lit up. He looked Hawk up and down appraisingly, even pausing at the muscles in his arms folded defiantly across his iron-pumped chest.

What the fuck? Dalton was checking him out? Was Pretty

Boy one of those don't-ask, don't-tell men? *Shit*. What the hell was Hawk supposed to do about that?

Since Hawk had always been a straight shooter, as well as straight, he decided to come right out with it. "Listen, you're free to live your life however you want, but please tell me you're not hitting on me. Because I gotta tell you, you couldn't be barking up a more wrong tree if you tried."

After a second of surprised silence, Dalton broke out laughing so hard he had to sober himself up before he could respond.

"No, Hawk. You're a real buff guy and all, but I'm as straight as you are and I've got a preg—uh—pretty girlfriend back home in the States to prove it. So no, we're not betting for a date with you." Dalton paused to chuckle one more time over that, then continued, "But I did just think of a really good wager."

If they weren't betting for Hawk's masculine virtue, then what? "What you got in mind, Dalton? Out with it."

"There's this, um, special assignment that needs filling. It requires just the right man. Let's say that if your side loses, you have to take it, no questions asked." Dalton appeared rather pleased with himself.

Hawk frowned. "If this assignment is so special, why haven't you already filled it? Why doesn't anyone else want it?"

"I didn't say no one wanted it, just that it's special and needs the absolute perfect soldier to fill it. Believe it or not, Hawkins, that might just be you."

"Well, I'm glad we both agree that I'm a perfect soldier, but I'm also on my way to Afghanistan for a year," Hawk reminded him. Probably more like eighteen months the way things had been going lately. "Tell me this, if we lose, which isn't likely, how could I possibly fulfill this assignment while deployed?"

"Easy. No problem at all. You can complete it before you go. Hell, you could probably even do it in Afghanistan if necessary. It's a quick one. A day. Two at most."

"You'll have to give me a little more information than that. I'd have to clear this with higher up the chain of command first."

What the fuck could this be about?

"Nope. No more info until the exercise is over and all the details for the assignment are ironed out. Besides, it'll be so much more fun for both of us if it's a surprise." Dalton tilted a head toward the bank of laptops. "I'm sure Matt can get it cleared with your superiors by the time we get off that mountain, *if* you're game that is."

Coleman could get it approved with Hawk's commanding officers? How the fuck was that possible?

Maybe it wasn't. This could all be a load of crap, in which case Hawk could agree to just about anything now and his superiors could shoot it down later, getting Hawk off the hook should he lose.

Even so, Hawk still had a nagging feeling he might have gone insane when he decided to agree to gamble for this unknown assignment. "Oh, I'm game, Dalton. Not that we're going to lose, but I'll accept your little wager. One question remains however. What do I get if, no, *when* we win?"

"I'm sure your winning won't be an issue." Dalton smiled. "But just to be fair, what would you like?"

That question stopped Hawk dead in his pride-filled shoes. "What do you mean, what would I like?"

"Exactly that. No games, Hawkins. If the universe shifts, hell freezes over, pigs fly and your group wins, what do you want?"

Cocky bastard. He'd show him. But still, Hawk couldn't come up with a thing.

"I don't know, " he admitted after an embarrassingly long moment spent in indecision.

Shit, why couldn't he think of anything really good?

A keg of beer crossed his mind, but didn't seem like enough compared to the mystery assignment he'd have to take in exchange.

A Humvee perhaps? Dalton had said *anything*, but what the

hell would he do with it while he was deployed. Not to mention that when he finally got back Stateside, Hawk had a feeling if he never stepped foot inside one of those vehicles again it would be too soon.

"Want a suggestion?" Dalton asked after watching Hawk struggle.

"Sure." What the hell. Might as well see what Pretty Boy had to say.

"*If* Zeta loses, I'll get you a tryout for the teams."

Hawk didn't miss the smirk on Dalton's face as he emphasized the word *if*.

He raised a brow and then purposely played dumb. "What teams?"

"You know what teams." The words *smart ass* were unspoken but unmistakably present in Dalton's response.

Hawk had to smile. He was enjoying sparring with Pretty Boy.

"So, do we have a deal? " Dalton asked, one pretty brow raised.

David Hawkins in the SpecOps? Never. Not gonna happen, but it might be fun to see what the tryout was like. It would sure make a hell of a story if he made it and then turned them down.

After a breath, Hawk nodded and shook Dalton's extended hand. "Deal."

Dalton turned to leave when Hawk stopped him. "Hey, Dalton. Tell me one thing."

Pretty Boy paused. "Yeah?"

"This assignment. Is it something you'd be willing to do yourself?"

"You worried, Hawkins?" Dalton laughed.

"Not worried. Just curious."

"Mmm hmm. Sure. But yeah, I've already done it. Believe me, I've already done it." Dalton turned to head for his task force commander, but not before looking back. "Oh, and Hawkins, besides the comm units, we've all got GPS implants too. So Matt can keep us informed of our positions during our real-world missions. I probably shouldn't have told you that either, but I figure your boys can use all the help you can get. See you up on the mountain."

Implanted tracking devices too? Well, fuck.

With that less than heartening farewell, the entire Task Force Zeta team disappeared as quickly as they'd arrived. He presumed they'd get into place on the mountain and await the arrival of Hawk's squad, who'd be walking into a pre-planned, computer-coordinated ambush like lambs to a slaughter.

Special assignment, here I come.

Double fuck.

~ * ~

"Pettit! Report!" Pinned down by Zeta's gunfire for the past hour, Hawk had never felt so disconnected from his men nor as helpless as he did right then. Dalton's team seemed to be everywhere, and always one step ahead of Hawk and his men.

"Four of Alpha team are down." Pettit's voice finally filtered through Hawk's earpiece. Hawk barely heard his Alpha-team leader over the noise, but what he'd heard wasn't good.

"Wally, what's Bravo team's status?" Hawk needed some good news at this point but there was no answer. "Wally. Dammit. Answer me!"

"I'm not allowed to talk if I'm dead, Hawk." Barely audible, Wally's voice came across the airwaves.

Shit.

More frustrated than before, Hawk shouted into his radio, "Bravo team. Someone who isn't dead, give me a damn report."

Radio silence gave him his answer. As far as this exercise was concerned, the entire Bravo team was deceased. That left himself and Pettit as sole survivors of his eleven-man squad. "Pettit?"

"Yeah, Hawk?"

"What's your location?"

"I'm behind the rocks just to the east of you."

"What do you say if we're going to go out, we go out with a bang?"

"You talking about the Butch and Sundance offensive defense?" Pettit always was quick to catch on. This time his guess was right on the money.

Butch Cassidy and the Sundance Kid, the squad's favorite movie. It was a classic. Sure, Butch and Sundance die, but they do it with style.

"That's exactly what I'm thinking, Pettit."

"Roger that. I'm ready."

He could hear the smile in Pettit's response. Doing something, even running toward your pretend death in a training exercise, was preferable to doing nothing at all.

"On my count of three. One." Hawk checked his ammo before continuing. "Two. Three!"

Hawk flung himself out from behind the rocks, dove and rolled behind the closest cover. When the shots came at him again, he was in better position to see exactly where they came from and how best to get there.

Aware of Pettit falling almost immediately to enemy fire to his left, Hawk lobbed a grenade in the direction of the incoming volley that had taken his team leader out. While that explosion kept the shooter down, Hawk ran full out, head on toward the shooter, jumped on top of the rocks hiding his opponent and showered the man hidden there with a hail of gunfire before feeling the hit in his own back.

Even with the knowledge that he was, for the purposes of this exercise, dead and a loser, Hawk felt satisfied. If nothing else at least he'd taken one of them out with him.

When he looked closer and saw it was Pretty Boy, he felt even better.

"Game over." Hawk smiled at the surprised and paint-splattered Dalton.

Barely a beat passed before Dalton nodded. "Yes, it is, Hawkins. Matt, make sure Hawkins has those orders for his special assignment waiting for him when he gets back to the garrison."

Pretty Boy flashed his pearly whites.

Hawk had temporarily forgotten about that damn special assignment. He stifled a groan.

Shit.

CHAPTER FOUR

Emily walked into the office and found Katie cradling the receiver and practically cooing into the phone. There was no doubt in her mind who was on the other end of that call. People in love could be so annoying. Cute, but annoying.

As she sat at her desk and proceeded to boot up her laptop, Emily noticed that even though Katie continued her conversation with BB, at least her boss had the decency to quit the lovey dovey stuff in deference to the lack of privacy.

"I told Em about the baby . . . Mmm, you're right. It probably is smartest to start transferring a few things sooner rather than later . . . I will, I swear."

Unashamedly, Emily listened to the half of the conversation she could hear. After all, her name had been mentioned. That made it okay. Right?

The printer across her and Katie's shared office began to buzz and spew out a few pages.

The part of Emily's brain that wasn't eavesdropping found that odd. Katie's computer wasn't even turned on and Emily had yet to open any files, let alone print them. But she was too intrigued by what Katie and BB would be transferring sooner rather than later to worry much about the printer.

Were BB and Katie moving so they could be together full time? And if so, where? More importantly, what did that mean for Emily and her job here in New York?

"It's here. Tell him I got it." The phone conversation continued. "Have fun going out tonight and safe flight home, baby, in case I don't get to talk to you before you leave . . . I love you too. Bye."

Emily noticed the tears in Katie's eyes as she hung up the phone. "You okay?" she asked.

Katie glanced up. "I'm fine. It's just the hormones. I can't even say goodbye without crying over it. Someone should really warn women that being pregnant also makes you insane."

Emily laughed. "I'll keep that in mind." Then she couldn't wait any longer to ask the question uppermost in her mind. "What are you going to do? I mean, where will you live once the baby is born and you get married? Down south near the base for his job, or here in New York so you can keep working? Or are you going to keep up the long-distance thing?"

Katie shook her head. "With the baby, a long-distance relationship would be ridiculous. But I can't expect him to give up his career for me."

"And he would never ask you to give up your career for him," Emily added.

"Exactly." Katie nodded.

Knowing her boss the workaholic would probably shrivel up and die if she wasn't able to work anymore, Emily could appreciate Katie's difficult decision. Of course, motherhood could change things.

"So what then?" Emily asked.

"Well, I kind of have a plan for that. It seems like we've picked up a lot of business in the south, especially with the latest military-recruitment ad campaigns. I'm thinking about suggesting opening a southeast branch. I could still fly to New York whenever necessary, but home base would be down south."

Emily hesitated before nodding. "Okay. I can do the south. My hair will frizz, but otherwise I won't miss the New York cold winters, or the outrageously expensive rent and super-sized cockroaches."

Katie smiled. "Thanks, Emily, but don't start packing yet. If I'm able to go full term with the baby, if the bosses agree to this and if I move—so many *ifs*—but if this all ends up happening, you don't have to follow me, you know. You can stay here in New York and continue to work."

"You don't want me to come with you?" Surprise and hurt colored Emily's voice.

"Of course I want you with me. I'd be lost without you. But you're getting too experienced for the job of my assistant. You need to start taking on clients of your own. The day will come when you'll be able to totally replace me, I'm sure."

Emily had been solely responsible for organizing absolutely every minute of Katie's daily life and holding down the fort at the office while she was away on her many business trips or visiting BB. Katie was so focused on work she would probably forget to eat if BB or Emily didn't remind her. That concern alone kept Emily pretty busy.

In addition, Emily was sometimes responsible for handling the talent—fetching non-fat lattes or bottled sparkling imported water for the models they dealt with for their marketing firm. But thinking about all the clients, bosses, divas, bitches and crap that Katie dealt with daily, Emily cringed at the thought of taking it all on herself.

"I'm not sure I'm qualified to totally replace you quite yet."

"Oh, you're qualified. You better be, because I'm about to give you your very first big solo assignment."

Big solo assignment?

Emily peered at Katie to confirm she'd heard correctly. "You're giving me a solo assignment?"

Katie grinned and nodded. "Mmm, hmm. It was initially BB's idea actually. He's worried about my working too hard when I travel. But I'm in total agreement with his suggestion on this one."

Travel? *Yay!*

Fears of divas and bitches forgotten, Emily sat up a little

straighter now. "For real? You'd trust me all alone with a client?"

Katie shook her head. "Why in the world are you so surprised?"

Emily opened her eyes wide. "Uh, because you're a control freak, for one thing."

Katie's mouth screwed up at the truth of that statement. "Maybe I was a little bit before."

"You think?" Emily couldn't help the sarcasm.

"Hey. Do you want this assignment or not?" Katie raised one perfectly shaped auburn brow in warning.

"Yes. And I'm sorry. You are the perfect boss, control issues and all." Emily pasted on an overly sweet smile.

"Well, I am also a pregnant control freak and I'm thinking a trip to Germany, if not Afghanistan, isn't the best idea right now."

"Germany or Afghanistan?"

Katie nodded in response.

Emily had to wonder what this assignment was. She let out a breath. "All right. That's okay. I like travel. I'm ready for anything."

Maybe not quite ready for Afghanistan, but she'd worry about that later.

Katie laughed while shuffling through a pile of papers and file folders on her desk. "I certainly hope you are ready, because I'm afraid it might not be easy."

God, Emily hoped she wouldn't be stuck working with some German-speaking model on this assignment. She could get by with a few words of French, even Italian, but German?

"Ah ha." Katie must have found whatever she had been looking for. "Here you go."

Emily's eyes opened wide as her boss thrust a file into her hands.

"US Army Marketing Campaign." Emily read the label aloud. An uncontrollable smile spread across her face as visions of soldiers danced in her head.

"I'm not sure you should be so happy about it." There was

31

concern in Katie's tone.

"Why not? You met and fell in love with BB during the Special Ops Recruitment Ad Campaign."

Katie nodded. "Yes. That I did."

"And we'll be using an actual Army guy for the shoots, just like we used BB because he's a real Special Operative for the last one?"

"Yes."

The joy nearly bubbled out of Emily. She tried but didn't quite control the squeal of happiness that escaped her lips. No diva models of either sex for her first real assignment.

Nope. She was getting to work with one of Uncle Sam's finest of her very own. She was more than ready for that.

Maybe she would get to pick the guy. Emily imagined a long line of uniform-bedecked soldiers, dog tags jingling as they all waited to meet her approval. Having to meet dozens, maybe hundreds of men had to put the odds in her favor of finding the one for her.

The thought of stumbling upon fairytale love, the kind Katie and BB had found, had her smiling even broader until Katie's insistent head-shaking ruined her good thoughts.

"What?" Emily sounded whiny, but she hated having her fantasy ruined, especially by a woman who already had her own hero cast.

"I just don't think you should be daydreaming about this particular soldier."

This particular soldier?

Disappointment warred with anticipation within her. "You've already picked him?"

"Not me personally, but yes, he's been chosen."

Was that a smirk on Katie's face?

"Who chose him?" And he had better be right, not only for the ad campaign but also for her. And single. God, she hoped he wasn't married.

"BB picked him for us."

Emily considered Katie's answer a moment.

Former underwear model turned Special Operative turned

military-recruiting poster boy, BB Dalton was so good looking he bordered on beautiful. He must know some handsome guys in the military, right? Did really hot guys hang out together in packs the way gorgeous female models did?

In any case, being a former model himself, BB would know the importance of having the right look for the ad campaign. The model had to be attractive.

"Okay." Emily nodded slowly, still wondering why Katie was hesitant about this candidate.

It would all work out just fine. BB was the sweetest man on earth. The perfect gentleman. No way would he pick a jerk for Katie and Emily to work with. The happiness bubble returned.

Emily flipped open the folder and shuffled through the few papers inside. "Is there a picture in here?"

"Not in the client folder, no. The model was a, uh, recent decision. Actually, I'm not considering it's a done deal yet. BB said he's one hundred percent sure he'll be the one, but the guy hasn't even received the information for the assignment yet. He'll get it when he gets back to his garrison tomorrow. Until he gets the orders, I'm not convinced he won't back out." Katie shrugged. "We'll know for sure soon, I guess."

Emily pouted with the nearly useless file in her hand. "So there's no information on him at all?"

Katie smiled. "Relax. Check the printer."

"The printer?"

"Matt, BB's computer-genius friend, sent a few background documents directly to our printer."

"How the heck?"

Katie shook her head. "Honestly, I don't know how he did it. Quite frankly, I think I don't want to know how Matt hacked into our wireless network from Europe and sent a document directly to our printer."

Emily glanced at the printer. Katie was probably right. Some things were better left unasked.

"I think there might be a picture of our potential model there," Katie continued.

That sent Emily flying across the room. She skidded to a stop and grabbed the pages waiting for her there in the printer tray.

She flipped through. "Damn. There's no picture, but there is a spec sheet. Staff Sergeant David Hawkins."

Mmm. That was a nice name. Emily Hawkins. Emily Price Hawkins. Staff Sergeant and Mrs. David Hawkins.

She continued reading. "He's thirty years old and seventy-two inches tall. That's . . ."

Emily squinted at the ceiling, doing the math until Katie interrupted her effort. "Six feet."

Excellent. Emily liked tall men. He'd look nice next to her five-foot-five-inch frame even when she wore heels.

"Hazel eyes. That's good. If we put him in Army green, it will bring out any green tint in his eyes for the photos." Her head spun with the possibilities.

"Really, Em. I don't think you should expect too much."

Emily frowned at Katie. "What aren't you telling me?"

The big sigh her boss released, accompanied by her guilty look, did not bode well.

"Emily, the soldier selected may not exactly be happy about this assignment."

"Is that all? You told me BB wasn't happy when he was ordered to do the recruitment campaign either, and that worked out fine."

More than fine. Katie had never been happier since meeting BB.

Nope. Emily was not about to abandon her dream of happiness because of one disgruntled soldier pouting over a photo shoot. She'd win him over fast enough and prove to Katie she could handle a big, supposedly difficult, assignment all on her own.

Big. Mmm. Most likely her soldier was big and muscular, as well as tall and handsome. This day was turning out pretty great and it was still only morning.

"I just wish there was a picture." Pouting, she looked accusingly at the printer . . . and noticed the blinking red light.

The machine was out of paper.

"Oh my God. There are more pages." Flying into action, Emily nearly ripped off one short, pale pink-polished fingernail tearing into a fresh ream of paper. She loaded it into the printer tray.

Tapping her foot while Katie laughed at her across the room, Emily waited impatiently for the next page to print.

"Come on, come on." She watched the printer, which was obviously not listening to her judging by how slowly it chugged along. Emily glanced up at her boss with frustration. "This is taking forever. We need a new printer."

Katie smiled indulgently but did get up to walk over and wait with Emily.

Finally, a color photo emerged ever so slowly from the machine. Close-shorn dark hair appeared first, followed by serious, piercing eyes. There was a strong, square chin and then a chest so broad and forearms so thick they could have easily belonged to a lumberjack.

David Hawkins's features would never be considered perfect like BB's. Instead, he was ruggedly handsome and all manly man. BB had chosen the quintessential warrior to represent the US Army.

Emily started grinning before the printing finished. Eyes never leaving the photo, she asked, "When do I meet him?"

CHAPTER FIVE

First was the humiliation of having to hike down the mountain alongside Task Force Zeta as they relived each and every kill among themselves. Sometimes they even stopped to enlighten Hawk and his men as to what Hawk's squad had done wrong during the mock slaughter.

Then Hawk had the pleasure of having to, while still wearing the game-ending paintball stain on his back, meet with Commander Miller once again back at the base camp. Miller had apparently watched and listened to every step of his golden boys' victory courtesy of Matt Call-Me-Computer-God Coleman.

Now the topper at the end of one hell of a shitty day—having drinks with Zeta. It was an invitation from Miller that Hawk thought best not to refuse even though the dead last thing he wanted to do was bond with frigging Task Force Zeta and discuss the exercise.

At least they'd gotten to eat some chow first. Hawk definitely could not have faced this on an empty stomach.

"Losing is more important than winning, if you learn from your mistakes." Jimmy Gordon delivered that advice in a southern drawl so thick, Pennsylvania-born Hawk nearly needed a translator to interpret for him.

"When you're done here, we can go over with you exactly

what you did wrong." Gordon had the nerve to make that offer while smiling and truly looking like he meant every frigging friendly word.

Hawk didn't want to talk to any one of them, but the beer at the pub was German, dark and strong, and the pool table actually had all of its balls.

All in all, since they couldn't fly out until morning, this might not be such a bad way to spend an evening, if he didn't have to sit here and listen to Zeta recap what he and his men had done wrong.

They didn't do anything fucking wrong. He wanted to shout that at them. They were outmaneuvered by technology, nothing more. That sucked, but worse, it scared the shit out of him.

"Hawkins?"

Leaning against the pool table, sighting his next shot, Hawk didn't even look up at Miller when he bit out a most likely less than polite, "What?"

Hawk finally glanced up in time to see the training commander's smirk. "Nothing. Just you're about to sink a striped ball."

"Yeah, so?"

Miller raised a brow. "So, you're solids, not stripes."

Shit. With a deep sigh, Hawk stepped back from the table, planted the cue stick on the ground and hung his head.

"What's wrong, son?"

The last thing he wanted to do was admit to Miller what he was about to, but he was a real man and so he would face reality.

"That loss to Zeta today shook my confidence. I mean, when I said I wanted Zeta to play full out I didn't realize what that meant. The implants, the computers . . . we're not ready."

Hawk looked at Miller and told him, with as much conviction as he could put into his voice, the absolute truth.

"We're not ready for Afghanistan. If the insurgents come at us with anything like Zeta did today . . ." Hawk shook his head and continued his confession, "What if I can't bring them home alive? What happens when all that red in the snow isn't paintballs but our blood? What if my men fall in those mountains in Afghanistan just like they all fell to Zeta today?"

"They won't." Miller spoke with a confidence Hawk could only wish he felt.

"But—"

"No *but* about it. Do you really think the Taliban has access to the kind of training and equipment our teams have?" Miller asked.

"They might."

"They don't."

"How do you know?"

"It's my job to know. And besides that, we've faced them, right there in their own backyard. I can't tell you much more except that our teams aren't always focused on training. A few years ago, I led Zeta personally into those exact mountains where you're headed and beyond them, and I brought them all back out again. Alive. And if you repeat what I just told you, I'll deny every word."

Hawk couldn't care less that Miller and his SpecOps had sometime in the past most likely trespassed in a country they shouldn't have been in. He was more worried about his guys and keeping them alive. But at least now the close, easy camaraderie between Miller and Zeta made more sense. They'd been together for a long time and they'd been through things he likely couldn't even imagine.

"No disrespect, sir, but with those men and that equipment I'm not surprised you and Zeta all came out alive. Unfortunately I've only got my normal, human men and crap for equipment."

"First, the guys on Zeta are regular men just like you. When you stop wallowing and get to know them better, you'll find that out."

When Miller chastised, he pulled no punches. Hawk bit his tongue to keep himself silent after the wallowing comment, true though it may be.

"Second, I can tell you this about what you're walking into in Afghanistan. The remaining Taliban factions survive only because of a thriving drug trade. If they were based anywhere else besides in the largest poppy-producing region in the world, they'd have little to no funding and be totally screwed."

Miller continued undeterred, "I'll concede that works in their favor. However, they're also in a region in constant turmoil. It's occupied by foreign powers but ruled by a newly created government as well as, unofficially, by the local warlords and tribal elders. Having too many heads like that leads to confusion and anarchy. Sometimes that climate will help the insurgents get a rare but small victory, but ultimately it leads to their defeat."

"How?" Hawk frowned. Those sounded like the perfect conditions for the bad guys to thrive.

"Their own allies turn on them, when they're not turning on each other. Most of the Taliban is living in squalor and chaos in those mountains. And believe me, they don't have anyone like our Matt Coleman designing their equipment."

The mention of Coleman aside, Hawk listened closely as Miller spoke. Now that he knew the man had been there, his words held more weight, though he said nothing that Hawk didn't to some degree already know.

"You and your men are good, Sergeant Hawkins. You held your own better and for far longer than I anticipated today. You'll have the advantage in those mountains. Trust me."

"Yes, sir." Hawk managed a nod, whether he believed it deep down or not.

"I've had about enough of chasing balls around a table. How about a beer?" Miller offered.

Now that was one thing Hawk could totally agree with Miller on, especially since the man was buying. "Yes, sir. I'd love one."

But once Hawk was leaning against the bar, strategically placed there by Miller, he realized Miller's sudden craving for beer had nothing to do with thirst and everything to do with throwing him in the path of Zeta's *normal* guys just to prove his point.

Miller introduced him to a dude named John Blake— no rank or service branch specified, Hawk guessed these guys were above that—and then Miller disappeared.

"So you're an Army staff sergeant." Blake shook his head with a laugh.

Hawk had noticed Blake's grin when Miller had mentioned Hawk's branch and rank during the introduction. It seemed to still amuse the guy. Hawk decided he'd had about enough for today without this guy and his attitude too.

Hawk straightened his spine, his knuckles whitening around his beer. "Yeah. What about it?"

Blake shrugged. "It's just that not too long ago I was you. I was Army Staff Sergeant John Blake. I was a tank commander in Ramadi."

"Ramadi. I'd heard things were pretty bad there." With more respect for Blake, Hawk decided to give him a pass. The cold beer sliding down his throat didn't hurt his newfound generosity either.

"Bad is an understatement." Blake laughed. "We were eyeball deep in snipers at camp to the point we couldn't even eat in the chow hall without body armor. A month before I left, I watched one of my men get hit with a vehicle-borne IED right in front of my eyes while he was dismounted. He was out of that tank following my orders. Good thing he's got a hard head and lived."

Blake shook his head again and took a sip of his beer. "And now look where I am and what I'm doing. I've got more shit implanted in my body than I ever knew existed, and I'm running around in the Alps playing what's probably the most expensive game of paintball on earth. What a difference a few months can make."

"You're trying to tell me a few months ago you were just a normal Joe out there in the sandbox?" Hawk frowned.

Blake nodded. "Yup. It was my third, and I guess my final

tour."

"So what happened? How did they get you?"

He laughed. "You make it sound like they took me hostage and brainwashed me or something. Like an alien abduction."

Exactly. All the Zeta guys had a bit of that Stepford-wife quality to them. Too perfect, too coordinated, too in tune with each other. As if they were humans replaced by robots, just like in that movie.

"I find it hard to believe that they pluck totally average guys out of the theater and turn them into you super soldiers."

Blake shrugged. "I can't speak for the rest of them, but in my case, yeah, believe it."

"So you're honestly trying to tell me you're all regular guys, just like me, but with better toys?"

At that, Blake laughed out loud. "Yeah, they—I mean *we* do have some pretty amazing toys, half of which Coleman over there invented. Now, he's not normal. He's an honest to goodness card-carrying genius."

When Hawk still wasn't convinced, Blake continued, "Look, I'm not saying any one of the troops out there would be right for the teams. Of course they're more selective than that. You have to have excellent basic skills as well as certain qualities. The ability to work in a group or alone. The aptitude to both lead or follow, and to switch between the two on a moment's notice."

"And that's it?"

"Well, no. It helps to be a language expert like Trey Williams over there. Or be able to drop a man with your bare hands like Jack Gordon. Or never miss a shot like Jack's brother, Jimmy Gordon. Or be a bomb expert like Bull Ford, or a diving and swimming champion like BB Dalton."

Yeah, Hawk got the idea. All perfectly regular guys. Sure. He snorted out a laugh.

"Okay, yeah, a lot of the guys used to be what you'd consider elite. Rangers. Delta Force. BB was a SEAL. But not me. I was just a tanker." Blake shrugged.

"So then why you? They all have specialties. What's yours?" Hawk asked.

Blake smiled. "I asked Miller that exact question when he mysteriously showed up at camp in Ramadi one day. He made quite an impression, I can tell you that, dressed head to toe in his black body armor."

"And?"

"He said I had an instinct. Some innate ability to think like the bad guys, and that was as valuable a skill as any of the others." Blake shrugged again as if he had trouble believing it himself.

"I've been told I have that instinct in me." Hawk wasn't one to brag, but both superiors and guys he'd served with had said that about him.

Staying one step ahead of the baddies was a skill that had kept him and his men alive more than once. Or perhaps it was just dumb luck. At this point, Hawk wasn't so sure anymore.

Blake nodded. "I know you do. I saw it today during the exercise."

Hawk let out a bitter laugh. "You mean the slaughter."

"It's all in the toys, Hawkins. Just the toys." Blake smiled and raised his beer to salute Hawk.

Against his will, Hawk smiled along with him. But God help them all if Miller was wrong and the bad guys got their hands on those toys too.

He was still smiling when Dalton appeared at his side. "So, Hawkins. Your assignment is all set and approved."

That information chased the short-lived humor right out of him.

Blake, looking amused, turned to Dalton. "You're really going to make him go through with that?"

Pretty Boy bobbed his head. "Damn right, I am. A bet is a bet. It's all set up and ready to go."

Hawk glared at Blake. "You know what this is about?"

"Oh, yeah. He wanted me to do it originally, but

apparently I'm not right for it now that I'm no longer enlisted Army. Not that I was going to do that shit anyway."

"If the commander told you to do it, Blake, you'd do it. Believe me. How do you think I got roped into it last year? The commander ordered me."

Hawk had the sudden urge to rip his hair out of his own head. "What is this *it* you're both talking about? Come on, Dalton. I lost. I admit that. I'll take the stupid assignment, but you at least have to tell me what it is."

"The orders will be waiting for you back at Hohenfels." Pretty Boy said it with a warning glance at Blake. The look said he better not spill the beans in the meantime.

Why was everyone being so mysterious?

"Hey, Hawkins? You got a girl?" a new voice coming from somewhere behind Dalton asked.

What the hell did his love life have to do with anything, and who the fuck was asking? Leaning past Dalton so he could identify the speaker as the computer god himself, Hawk frowned. "No. Why?"

"Because after this assignment, you will." Matt Coleman joined their conversation uninvited. "Maybe too many of them. Not too long ago, the team had to physically protect BB here from his adoring female fans at a bar. Of course, that wasn't such a chore. Especially the one who took her shirt off so he could sign her tits."

Fans? Adoring female fans ripping their clothes off? Hawk glanced at Blake, who shrugged. "Don't look at me. That was before my time."

"So anyway, Hawkins, I wanted to say good job today." The computer god actually sounded sincere.

Reminded again of the loss, and that Matt Coleman and his computers were the cause of it, Hawk scowled. "Yeah, thanks."

"No, really. I mean it. If I didn't have your entire squad mapped with thermal satellite images so I was able to tell our boys your exact locations, you might have had a chance."

Thermal satellite images. Crap. The word *cheaters* sprang to

Hawk's mind again as he let out a disgusted sigh before taking another gulp of his beer.

"Toys, Hawkins. Just toys." Blake grinned once again.

Hawk was starting to really hate these boys and their toys.

CHAPTER SIX

On the flight to Germany, Emily read and reread every document in the file Katie had given her—the plans and goals for the marketing campaign and, more importantly, the information about David *Hawk* Hawkins. BB had supplied them with the soldier's nickname, but there was scarce little else she knew about him. What there was, she devoured eagerly.

Too excited to really concentrate on anything, Emily totally ignored both the paperback novel she'd bought at the airport shop and Jai Devereaux, the photographer on the assignment with her. Out of guilt, Emily finally turned the book over to Jai to read on the long, boring overseas flight.

When Katie had rushed to schedule phase one of the campaign, the photo shoot, for as soon as possible, Emily hadn't argued. For some reason, Katie was convinced that if they didn't get it done soon, Hawk would back out and they'd have to find a replacement.

Emily's motives for the rush were very different.

She'd scrambled to secure both a photographer and plane tickets and had done so incredibly fast. Just days after BB had chosen Hawk, Emily was in the air and on the way to meet him in Germany.

Hawk. God, she loved that nickname. It was so manly. She

45

glanced down at the file for the thousandth time. Staff Sergeant David S. Hawkins. Aka Hawk.

Oh, yes. A man with a name like that brought to mind all sorts of images and possibilities, and Emily considered each and every one of them repeatedly throughout the flight. And during the wait for the luggage. And on the drive to Hohenfels, where she hoped her dreams would finally come true.

"How long until we get there?" It was the second time during the drive from the airport she'd asked that question, but she couldn't help herself. She was as excited as a kid on Christmas morning.

Behind the wheel of the rental car, Jai raised one dark eyebrow and glanced at her sideways. "Anxious to get there, are we?"

She may have known Jai for two years now and worked with him on countless of Katie's marketing campaigns, but that didn't mean she told him everything. No way was she willing to divulge her true hopes for this shoot—the real reason her hand shook as she held the file she'd once again taken out.

Prince Charming was just miles, or rather kilometers, away now. And after studying him on paper for days, Emily was already half in love with him.

"Of course, I'm anxious. This is the first solo assignment Katie's ever trusted me with."

"Yeah, about that. How did you get her to do that? She's usually totally hands on."

"Don't you mean a control freak?"

Jai's dark face broke into a grin. "Yeah. So what happened?"

Emily bit her tongue about the pregnancy. That wasn't her news to tell, so she shrugged. "I guess she thinks I'm ready."

She hoped her boss was right.

"You'll do fine." Jai's dreadlocks swung as he pivoted his head to glance at her and then turned quickly back to the road.

A car right on their tail flashed its lights and then sped by them in the oncoming lane of traffic. Damn, people drove fast here in Germany. Emily was certainly glad Jai had offered to take the wheel.

Once she could breathe again after the near traffic disaster, she decided to try and get some work done during the remainder of the trip. "I've got some ideas for shots."

"Great. Shoot." Jai grinned at his own little joke.

Rolling her eyes, Emily couldn't help but smile herself. "I've been considering what to have Hawk wear. I guess we have to get a few of him in his dress uniform. But I really want a bunch of pictures in those cute camouflage pants too."

"Of course. I totally agree. Camo was all over the runways in Milan and Paris this season."

"I know." Excited, it wasn't until she saw Jai's smirk that Emily realized he was teasing her.

"Sorry, Em. Couldn't resist." Jai winked in answer to her scowl. "Go on. What else did you have in mind?"

Glancing at the death grip Jai had on the steering wheel as another car honked and whizzed past, rocking both them and the vehicle, Emily decided the rest could wait. "Let's see what we find when we get there. We might get more ideas on site."

"Looks like you don't have long to wait now, because here we are."

Emily put down the folder and saw the high fence of the base coming into view. She felt her heart thud harder. No, there wasn't long to wait at all.

Jai slowed the car to a crawl as they neared the two armed, make that *very* armed, guards at the gate. He stopped and rolled down the window. "Jai Devereaux and Emily Price. We're here to photograph Staff Sergeant Hawkins. We're expected."

"Yes, sir. IDs, please."

"Got your passport handy?" Jai looked at Emily expectantly as he passed his own to the guard through the open window.

"Um, oh. Yeah. Hold on." Emily searched through her large and now rather unorganized carry-on and finally, after a brief moment of panic, found her passport in the side pocket. She handed it to Jai, who gave it to the scary guard for his intense scrutiny.

"I'll have to ask you both to exit the vehicle."

Panicked, Emily shot Jai a look. "What did we do? Are they going to search us?"

Oh my God. What if they strip-searched her? Was she wearing nice underwear? She couldn't remember.

"It's fine, Em. Just do as they say." Jai looked much calmer than she felt.

Emily stared at Jai, suddenly unable to move. "But—"

"Em. Trust me. Just get out of the car, please . . . and stop talking." Jai stared back as the armed and ready guards waited in stony silence for them to get out of the car.

Here was an unexpected wrench in Emily's fairytale scenario. Getting searched and thrown in a foreign prison by the guards at the gate.

The one guard who had moved to her side of the vehicle made Emily so nervous it took her two tries to get the door of the car open. When he told her to leave her bag inside, she nearly passed out from anxiety.

Airport security, she was used to. Stone-faced men with machine guns calling her *ma'am* as they ordered her about and searched her belongings was quite another.

Although the sun shone brightly, Emily wrapped her arms closer around herself to ward off both the cold air and the chill of fear.

After one guard had finished inspecting the front and back seats while the other one stood by and watched with weapon in hand, the first camouflage-clad soldier turned to Jai. "Please pop the trunk, sir."

While Emily decided men in camouflage uniforms might not be so sexy after all, Jai nodded and reached in to hit the button on the door. It released the latch on the trunk where they'd stowed their luggage and photographic equipment at

48

the airport.

Just as Emily decided she was going to call Katie as soon as possible and tell her she would never take another military assignment again, a soldier rushed toward them in a light jog.

Instinct had her taking a step back, until she noticed he was smiling and had his hand extended in greeting. The fact he wasn't armed with some kind of machine gun also helped calm her immensely.

"Miss Price." He shook her hand and then turned to Jai. "Mr. Devereaux. I'm Ryan Pettit. The captain sent me down to escort you."

Pettit watched as the guards replaced Jai's camera equipment carefully back in the trunk. "We send a soldier to meet any photographers and reporters and then, after a routine inspection of the equipment, we sign them in under our care."

Emily breathed for what seemed like the first time since they'd pulled up to the gate. Jai sent her a look that said, *I told you so*, but she still had no intention of apologizing to him for being worried. The entire experience had been nerve-wracking and she would definitely yell at Katie at the earliest opportunity for not warning her about base procedure.

After his short interaction with the guards that included a nod and very few words, Pettit turned to them. "We're good to go. I can ride in the backseat and direct you where to drive."

Just having him in the car made Emily feel better. Kind of like the guards would be less likely to shoot her if one of their own was seated directly behind her in the line of fire.

Pettit's smile and enthusiasm was infectious. Once out of view of the guardhouse, she began to relax.

"The captain didn't go into any detail except that you're here for a photo shoot. So what are you going to photograph?" Pettit leaned forward from the center of the back seat so he could both give Jai directions and talk to Emily.

Emily turned in her seat. "It's a new marketing campaign

to establish stronger branding for the US Army. We're hoping to raise public awareness and increase recruitment." She recited verbatim the goals Katie had developed for the campaign.

Pettit laughed. "Okay. Whatever you say. Turn right up here."

Jai nodded and did as he was told, driving at a snail's pace, which also helped to calm Emily's nerves after the hour and a half speed-of-light drive from the airport in Munich.

"I don't know much about marketing and stuff but branding means logos and slogans and things, right?"

She nodded. "Pretty much. Yeah."

"But the Army already has that. Army slogans are classic. *Be all that you can be. Army Strong.* They're great. Are you going to change it all?"

"No, just reinforce the message and make it stronger." Emily felt the need to reassure him since he seemed very attached to the slogans.

Pettit nodded. "How you going to do that? Make it stronger, I mean?"

"By giving the Army a face the people can relate to." *Hawk's face*, Emily thought. "One soldier that will represent all of you."

"Really? Cool. So who—oh wait. I missed the turn." Pettit interrupted his own question. "We'll have to turn left at this corner and then left again. It's the first building, right there on the corner. You can just park at the curb."

As soon as the car stopped, Pettit jumped out and opened Emily's door for her. Military guys were so polite. She got a tingle again in anticipation of meeting Hawk.

"I'll run in and tell the captain you're here then come back out and help you unload your equipment. Captain has a room cleared for you to set up in. You can leave your stuff there overnight if you want. It's secure." After relaying that information, Pettit trotted off and Emily had the opportunity to consider just how sweet soldiers were . . . at least the ones without guns who weren't searching her.

CHAPTER SEVEN

Hawk stared down at the large manila envelope lying on top of the blanket on his rack. He dropped the unopened letters he'd gotten during mail call onto the bed and reached for the envelope.

The moment he opened it and pulled out the paper, he knew what it was. Orders for Dalton's damn special assignment.

Sitting down heavily, he read over the duty he'd let Pretty Boy talk him into betting. When no orders had shown up immediately upon his return from the training in the Alps, Hawk had deluded himself into thinking this mystery assignment had been Dalton's idea of a practical joke.

No such luck. Even reading it again didn't change the contents.

"No. No fucking way." He shook his head and spoke out loud in his empty quarters.

"What's up, Hawk?" Wally poked his head through the open doorway.

Hawk glanced up at Wally. "Um, nothing. Just a, um, letter from home." He lied and folded the computer printout in thirds, hoping Wally would think it was a letter even though it looked far more like orders than mail.

"Everything okay?"

"Yeah, it's just um, a letter from my sister. She's dating some idiot. No big deal."

"She cute, your sister? Give her my address. We can be pen pals. I'll knock that other guy right out of her mind with my charm." Wally grinned wide.

"Yeah, right, because you would be a real improvement over her dating an idiot." Lie or not, Wally the womanizer dating Hawk's sister, or even being pen pals with her, was not going to happen. At least not during Hawk's lifetime.

"Damn right, I would. Besides, chicks love me. You got a picture of her?"

"Get out of here, Wally, and let me finish reading my mail."

"Just keep me in mind." With one final grin, Wally was gone.

Thank God, because Hawk had enough to deal with right now. The moment the coast was clear of Wally and his curiosity, Hawk headed out of the barracks to find someone of some authority. His sole goal was to get out of this assignment if it killed him.

There was no way he was going to do this. No way his superiors would make him do this. Why should he have to follow orders that Dalton and Coleman had somehow finagled?

After all, this wasn't a real assignment. He wouldn't be saving lives or even taking them but instead . . . Hawk shuddered at the thought of what he would be doing.

Fucking Dalton. No wonder he'd looked so smug about this mystery assignment, and it made total sense that he'd already done it himself. Damn white-toothed fancy boy probably enjoyed it too.

Thinking back to his last discussion with Pretty Boy and the Zetas—as he'd come to think of them—things started to make even more sense. Coleman's mention of the female attention Hawk would garner from this assignment. Blake saying he couldn't do it because he was no longer regular Army.

Fuck. He'd walked right into this. He would never, ever agree to something without knowing all the details again.

Hawk was shaking, vibrating with anger and tension by the time he got to the Head Shed. It was affectionately called that because the company commanders hung out there. As he had hoped, he found his own captain in the Company Orderly Room.

"Sergeant Hawkins. Pleasure to see you back."

"Yes, sir. Thank you. Captain, can I, uh, speak with you for a moment?"

Ignoring his request, Hawk's company commander turned to the other captain seated next to him. "Sergeant Hawkins and his guys had a little fun in the Alps with some of Hank's boys this past week. In fact, Hank called to compliment me on how exceptionally well the squad did during the training."

Hawk's brow rose. "Hank's boys, sir?"

"Yeah. Hank Miller. He was the training commander up there with you."

"Yes, Captain. I met him. I, uh, wasn't aware . . . You know him, sir?" And was on a first name basis, no less. Great. Just great.

"Oh, yeah. We were deployed together once upon a time, back when he was regular Army. Then he moved on to Delta Force, and from there, onto *the teams* as he calls the boys in black."

"I wasn't aware of that, sir. That's what I wanted to talk to you about, sir, the training and the, uh, other thing." Hawk held up the folded orders in his hand, wishing his company commander would ask the other captain in the room to leave so they could have some privacy.

No such luck. His commanding officer laughed.

"Oh, yeah. The special assignment." To Hawk's great dismay, his commander turned to his neighbor again. "You won't believe this. Sergeant Hawkins here has been chosen to be the face of the modern Army for some feel good marketing campaign. They figure by plastering his mug all over the press, everyone will get the warm and fuzzies about us and what we're doing."

"To what end?" The captain's cohort finally spoke, looking surprised.

"Increase awareness. Encourage recruitment. Enlighten folks to our efforts for stabilization and rebuilding. Supposedly they had a similar campaign for the SpecOps starring one of Hank's guys last year. Some former SEAL who had modeling experience prior to joining up, if you can believe that."

A SEAL on Hank's team with prior modeling experience. Yup, that had to be Dalton. He had been a male model? Hawk supposed he shouldn't be surprised by that.

He remembered Pretty Boy's exact words. *'I've already done it, Hawkins. Believe me.'*

This kind of assignment was fine for Dalton, but not for Hawk. He was a real soldier.

The captain went on, "That campaign was incredibly successful for recruitment and public relations. That's what Hank said when he sold the idea to me on the phone anyway."

So the miraculous appearance of Hawk's orders hadn't been all Dalton's doing. It had been Dalton's commander, Hank Miller, helping too. At least Hawk felt a bit better that Pretty Boy and his computer god, Coleman, weren't all-powerful.

The chances of Hawk getting out of this incredibly embarrassing and ridiculous assignment were looking slim. Still, he had to try. "Sir. That's what I wanted to talk to you about. I'm not some male model. I'm a trained soldier."

"Exactly. That's why they want you. They don't want a hired head. They want a real, battle-toughened warrior."

"Forgive my asking, sir. But have you seen the guy they used for the SpecOps ads? Because I have. He's some pretty boy who looks like he belongs in those perfume ads you see on television. I look nothing like that."

"Thank God for that. I don't want some delicate boy representing my Army." The captain shrugged. "The marketing people chose you, Sergeant. I have to trust they know what they're doing."

Bullshit. Dalton had chosen him out of spite, not some marketing expert. And how that all fit together—how Dalton got to choose the new face of the Army—Hawk still wasn't sure. Not that it mattered now. All that mattered was getting out of it.

"But how am I going to do this thing when I'm downrange? I'm deploying forward with my guys in a couple of weeks."

The company commander shook his head. "Not a problem. They're already here."

Here where? Here at the garrison, here? And who exactly was here? Hawk's heart jumped. Perhaps he'd misunderstood. Before totally panicking, he decided to clarify first. "Sir? Who's already where?"

"The photographer and the marketing person. I just got word from the gate that they've arrived. I sent Sergeant Pettit down to meet them and escort them here. In fact, they should have arrived by now."

Pettit? Oh, no, no, no, no.

How the hell was Hawk going to keep this thing a secret if Pettit knew? The teasing would be relentless. Soldiers never forgot. He'd have to live with this forever, until the day he died, which after this embarrassment would hopefully be soon.

Upon that thought, Pettit flew through the door. "Captain. Your civilians are here, sir."

Pulling Hawk aside, Pettit whispered with a smile, "Wait until you see this marketing chick from the States. Blonde. Cute."

Great. A woman no less. Hawk got to embarrass himself and play model in front of some blonde as well as his team leader Pettit. Just perfect.

Pettit, practically bouncing in his boots, turned back to the captain. "Sir. Miss Price was telling me about the ads. Do you know who they're going to use as their model?"

Hawk's hope grew. Pettit didn't know. Maybe there was still a chance.

The captain broke into a huge smile and all hope fled. "You're standing next to him, Sergeant Pettit."

Pettit's eyes opened wide as he looked at Hawk. "You mean Sergeant Hawkins, sir?"

With a disgusted sigh, Hawk nodded. "Yeah. It's me."

"Wow. My staff sergeant is going to be the face of the Army. How cool is that?" Pettit grinned, looking totally thrilled.

Hawk stifled a groan of dismay. "Yeah, great. Real cool."

Somewhere far in the distance, Hawk imagined he heard Dalton laughing.

CHAPTER EIGHT

"Staff Sergeant Hawkins. It's a pleasure to meet you." Inside the room they'd been assigned to use, Emily stepped forward and delivered the greeting she'd settled on and rehearsed in her mind during the flight over.

She smiled and tried to stop her hand from shaking as she extended it toward Hawk.

Hawk folded burly Popeye-like forearms across his chest. Emily lowered her hand.

She'd tried to be friendly. He met her overtures with what amounted to thinly veiled rudeness followed by one long glance that covered her from head to toe and all the parts in between.

Feeling exposed after that look, even in her cashmere turtleneck, wide-legged wool trousers and leather boots, she couldn't resist the urge to cross her arms over her chest. Boy, was she glad she'd chosen pants over a skirt. She didn't need him ogling her legs too.

Jai, apparently not going to make the same mistake at camaraderie that Emily had made, nodded from the corner as he continued to unpack the cameras and lights they'd carried in from the car. "I'll be photographing you today, Sergeant."

Silent and expressionless, Hawk nodded back.

Staff Sergeant David *Hawk* Hawkins was a lot of things,

and to Emily's vast and bottomless devastation, so far none of them were good.

Her heart fell. It felt as if Hawk had stomped on it, and her hopes, with one slam of his very large combat boots.

He had the muscles she'd dreamed of, but along with them came a truckload of testosterone-fueled bad attitude. He seemed every inch the serious warrior his picture had hinted at, but she sensed he was also as stubborn and unyielding as a mule. And just as much of an ass.

Were mules the same as asses? She wasn't sure, but Hawk was behaving like both.

The Neanderthal before her, the Hawk-man himself, waited with a stone-faced expression as Jai set up the equipment. But no, maybe he wasn't as stony as he appeared. Beneath the cold, steely exterior, Emily sensed molten anger bubbling just below the surface.

Maybe his attitude was just resistance to the assignment. Katie had warned her that could be the case.

In fact, Katie had been convinced Hawk would back out of it in the beginning. If he were that unhappy about this, it could account for the standoffishness.

It could be partially Emily's fault too. She was so used to working with sensitive, artistic, metrosexual straight guys or openly gay males that she simply didn't know what to do with a real manly man, an alpha male to the Nth degree, when she came across one.

Perhaps that was the problem with her dating life too. Something to think about . . . later. Right now she had an unhappy hulk of a male to handle. If only she could get him past this.

He was handsome in a rough and ready kind of way.

Hot too, with dark hair cropped close to his head, deep intense eyes that gave her a view into his emotions—which was not exactly a plus at the moment—and a body so big it would definitely let a woman know she was being held.

Emily picked her heart back up off the floor where it had first been trampled by Hawk's cold reception, dusted it off and tried to salvage both this assignment and her dreams.

"So I was thinking first we can take some shots inside using the plain backdrop Jai set up. That way I can superimpose different backgrounds for various ads as needed. Then, if it's still light enough, we can move outdoors and scout some locations for exterior action shots for tomorrow's shoot." Steeling her nerves, she made direct eye contact with him.

No comment.

Emily sighed. This wasn't going to be easy, but nothing worth doing was. She turned to her only ally in the room. "Jai? What do you think?"

Jai looked up from the light meter in his hand. "Huh? Oh, yeah. Sounds good, Em."

Turning back to Hawk, she let her gaze roam over him the way his had traveled up and down her before.

The fright from the guards a distant memory now, she was back to appreciating the benefits of a man dressed in camouflage. Even this man.

"We can shoot the camouflage outfit first, since you're already wearing it." Emily noticed one dark brow cock up. She paused and waited.

"Outfit?" Hawk scowled. "It's a uniform. An Army advanced combat uniform or ACU."

She felt her face pale at his censure. "Okay. Sorry."

This hadn't turned out at all the way she'd pictured in her dreams. In fact, it was becoming more and more like a nightmare.

Jai looked as if he was nearly ready, so Emily figured she'd better be brave and broach the next subject. "So we'd like to um . . . " How to say this without getting shot down again? "Make your, uh, physical form stand out in the photos."

There was that brow again, but this time accompanied by a smirk.

He remained silent, so she continued, "So maybe you could roll up the sleeves of your camouflage uniform shirt so we can see your arms a bit?"

Even though she'd remembered to call it a uniform and not an outfit—as if she would ever forget that again—she still got the disapproving look and head shake.

"No can do. And it's called a jacket, not a shirt."

Why couldn't he just do one little thing without being difficult as well as correcting her terminology? As if she should know what military clothes are called.

"Why can't you?" Emily widened her stance, ready for battle. He wanted to argue? She could argue.

"Because it's against the rules, that's why."

"But I swear I've seen guys with their sleeves—" The steady sway of his head still shaking at her finally stopped her in her tracks. "What?"

"You may have seen it, but it's against our regulations and I can't do it."

He meant *won't* do it. Emily couldn't imagine that his captain really gave a darn what his sleeves looked like.

"Maybe we can ask someone if it would be okay—"

He actually laughed at that. "No."

With a huff, she gave in.

"Fine. Are you allowed to take off your *jacket*?" Emily emphasized the word that he'd insisted on correcting her on. "Can you wear just your T-shirt for some photos or is that against the rules too?"

"Yes, I'm allowed."

Finally, a yes, but still he didn't move.

"Could you please take off your jacket?"

Hawk smirked but complied, thank God. With a chuckle, he took it off.

Now he was laughing at her? Emily planted her hands on her hips. "What's so funny?"

"It's been a long time since a woman ordered me to take my clothes off. Maybe this gig won't be so bad after all." Hawk hung what still looked more like a shirt than a jacket on the back of a chair and turned back to her. He paused with a hand on his nylon belt. "Pants too, doll?"

Doll?

She narrowed her eyes. "No, thanks. Maybe later."

Pig. Worst of all, a pig with bulging biceps and beautiful pecs beneath a very tight T-shirt. His dog tag chain nestled right between those delectable pecs.

Emily suddenly imagined him standing before her without the shirt. All big and burly.

What was she doing? He was such a . . . a . . . There were no words to describe him.

The chuckle from Jai's direction didn't help Emily's mood. She shot him a nasty look as well.

She turned back to Hawk and sighed. She had to get into a professional mindset. No more pouting that he wasn't Prince Charming. No more bickering because he was acting like the typical difficult model. She was used to that at least.

Thinking like Katie would, Emily imagined the finished print advertising. Hawk, standing in his T-shirt and camo pants. Arms crossed . . . make that hairy arms crossed.

Darn. BB was practically hairless but Hawk, no such luck. What were the chances of Emily being able to get him to wax the hair off his forearms?

And if they chose to do a few shirtless shots, would he wax his chest? Probably his back would require de-hairing, also.

Stifling a laugh at the ridiculous notion, she figured the odds of him agreeing were slim to none.

Could they airbrush out that much hair? And exactly how many tattoos were the tan T-shirt and camouflage pants hiding? Now that she was getting to know him better, he seemed the type to have ink, and lots of it. Probably a really crude naked lady or obscenities. Or maybe some morbid, bloody skull tattoo.

Emily could only guess. She and Katie hadn't discussed the possibility of tatts. They'd have to airbrush out any bad ones to keep the ads G-rated.

Moving on, a small detail she'd missed before hit her. She frowned. "Your shirt. It's tan."

"Yeah, so?"

"So, shouldn't it be green? You know, Army green. No?"

"No."

"Why not?"

"What do you mean why not?" He frowned and shrugged. "Just because. I don't know why. I don't make the rules."

"Oh, come on. I know I've seen military men in olive-green shirts."

He nodded. "I'm sure you have, but we wear tan T-shirts with our Advanced Combat Uniform."

She sighed again, deeper. Fighting the rules seemed useless, but she couldn't resist one last word. "Well, that tan does nothing to bring out the color of your eyes."

Hawk smiled broadly at that, looking genuinely amused, an emotion Emily had begun to doubt was in his repertoire.

"I'll make sure to point that out to my superiors. Maybe they'll consider changing the regulation uniform in deference to the color of my eyes."

Well, that was the highest number of syllables she'd heard come out of him all at once since meeting him.

Emily had a strong urge to stick her tongue out at him. He'd probably laugh at her for that too, so she didn't give him the satisfaction.

She heard Jai's shutter and looked up to see him snapping candid photos of Hawk, who went from laughing at her expense, to a frown, to looking stern and kind of scary in a matter of seconds.

"That's great, Sergeant." Jai wore a grin. "Perfect. I want your whole range of expressions over the next couple of days."

That led to an even more comical expression of horror clearly written across Hawk's face.

Had he just realized that whether he was happy about it or not, this photo shoot and this ad campaign starring him was going to happen?

Difficult or not, he was stuck with them and there was nothing he could do about it.

Now it was Emily's turn to smile.

CHAPTER NINE

With the hellish part of a day that he'd rather forget finally done, Hawk headed for his bunk, only to be waylaid by Wally at the door of their barracks.

"Hey, Hawk. We're heading out to get some beers. We figure we'd better get it while we still can since there'll be no drinking or anything else fun where we're going. Wanna come?"

He could sure as hell use a beer about now after what he'd just been through, but he couldn't go out on a bender and get drunk tonight. He had to get up early in the morning and meet with the cute and curvy but dim-headed marketing chick and her smart-ass Rastafarian photographer again.

Tomorrow they had to scout locations for exterior action shots and then shoot outside if the weather was good. They hadn't had enough light left to do it today.

Scouting locations and worrying about the light. Great, now he was starting to think like a frigging model.

"Nah. I'm heading to my room."

"Where the hell have you been all day, anyway?" Wally frowned as if he'd just noticed Hawk's extended and unexplained absence, just as Pettit walked up.

Hawk shot a quick warning glance at Pettit and answered Wally's question, "Special assignment."

Pettit froze where he was.

Hopefully the threats Hawk had levied against him in the captain's office that afternoon would keep Pettit's mouth shut and it would stay a *special assignment* as far as the rest of the squad was concerned.

He leveled Pettit one more stern look. His team leader, who obviously didn't comprehend how miserable Hawk was about the whole modeling thing, rolled his eyes behind Wally's back.

"Yeah? What kind of special assignment?" Wally continued relentlessly.

Hawk let out a short laugh. "The classified kind."

"Fine, whatever. We're leaving in thirty if you change your mind and decide you wanna come." Wally scowled and disappeared into his room.

Pettit slunk closer. "I don't understand why you—"

"My assignment. My choice."

After Hawk cut him off, his team leader sighed. "Fine, but if you think your face can be featured in every Army ad worldwide and no one will notice, you're crazy."

"And if you think we're gonna see any advertising in those mountains in Afghanistan, you're crazy. We'll be long gone by the time those ads hit, and a year from now or more, when we finally do come home, they'll have realized their mistake in using me and will have moved on to some other poster boy. Believe me." Hawk crossed his arms, certain his prediction would come true.

"For your sake, Hawk, I hope you're right." Shaking his head, Pettit turned toward his room.

Oh, Hawk would make sure he was right.

He'd be so unpleasant to work with, Goldilocks would ensure he'd never work on another assignment with her again. She'd go running looking for a new model. Dalton would just have to find her a new sucker for this job.

It was a damn shame too, to have to do that to her. She was a looker, if you liked them young and starry-eyed.

Hawk tended to go for the more experienced women. He

had neither the time nor the patience for innocent types like the bubbly blonde from today who had wanted him to roll up the sleeves of his camo *outfit* and wear a green shirt to match his eyes.

Shaking his head with a laugh at that memory, he pivoted toward his own room to get his beauty sleep and curse Dalton for the thousandth time that day.

Apparently modeling was harder work than it seemed judging by his exhaustion.

Quite simply, he was done in. Running through the Alps for two straight days had taken its toll on his body. And now his special assignment had done a real number on his brain too.

It all caught up with him at once. Sleep found him the moment his head hit his lumpy pillow.

"Take off your shirt, Hawk."

He did, and Goldilocks ran a brightly painted, long fingernail across his chest. He could feel her touch on his skin. It caused a shiver to shoot through him. Standing on tiptoe in her mile-high stilettos to reach his ear, she breathed, "I want you. Now."

She didn't need to ask him twice.

Hawk reached down and hoisted her up. She wrapped her legs around him. Beneath her miniskirt, he cupped each gloriously round, bare ass cheek her thong exposed.

Somehow, she freed his hard length from his pants. A slight shove had the thin string of her thong pushed to the side and him sliding easily into her. He groaned as a shudder ran through him.

She gripped his head with two hands, kissing across his face, his throat, his chin. When she reached his mouth, she slipped her tongue inside.

He could feel her body—tight, wet, hot—as she slid up and down his slick length.

"Harder, Hawk." She was demanding, insatiable as the muscles deep inside her began to grip and pulse around him.

She cried out, loud, unashamed, with each of his thrusts until he lost all control and came with her.

Breathing heavily, Hawk awoke alone in his bunk.

He'd been dreaming.

Hawk, who usually slept like a rock, had actually dreamed.

Not a nice, normal nightmare either, like forgetting to get dressed and attending a Promotions Board meeting in his underwear or anything like that. Oh, no. Thanks to Dalton and his little modeling assignment, Hawk's slumber had been visited by images more appropriate for triple-X films than his weary brain.

The sticky mess covering the spent erection in his boxer briefs was a much too real reminder of his shame.

But that was nothing compared to the knowledge that in mere hours he'd have to look Goldilocks in the eye and try not to remember how amazing it felt to be inside her, even if it had been only in his dreams.

Yeah, the way the two of them got along like oil and water, that was pretty much what she'd tell him should he ever suggest them hooking up—in his dreams.

Shit.

Hawk rose from his bed and headed to the bathroom to clean up. He needed to get laid for real and soon, before they deployed and all he'd have were his dreams.

CHAPTER TEN

Emily stirred real cream into her to-go coffee cup thinking how much she loved Europeans. No skim milk for these folks, unlike skinny-conscious Americans.

In the dim light of dawn, she watched the people bustling past the window. She and Jai were grabbing coffee near their hotel before heading back to Hohenfels.

The town nearest the US Army garrison had some surprisingly good coffee shops and restaurants.

Emily realized she was finally getting some of the military-speak down. She even knew what a garrison was now, and her uniform knowledge had been greatly increased after yesterday's photo session with Hawk.

She tried not to think about that.

The best part of yesterday had been at the end of the day when they'd gotten away from the garrison and Hawk's bad mood.

Emily and Jai had found a great spot to eat after that. They'd had a quick but sumptuous dinner before, jetlagged, they crashed early. The hotel wasn't bad either. Too bad she'd barely slept.

"Why did we decide to meet so early?" She tried not to sound too whiny then smothered a yawn.

"Because the Army starts their day early. And, because we

need to set up the shots and be ready to go when and if the sun finally comes out today." Jai looked up at the overcast sky darkening the pink-tinged sunrise. "I hope it doesn't snow."

So did Emily. It was bad enough that, though exhausted, she needed to be on her toes to handle Hawk. The last thing she wanted to deal with was snow during their outdoor shots. She had on her good leather boots.

She hated snow as much as the cold and early mornings. That was true no matter what time zone they happened to be in.

Sunrise. Honestly, she couldn't remember the last time she'd seen one of those.

Tired, dreading the day ahead and feeling a need for sugar as well as caffeine, Emily grabbed some sort of rich looking German pastry and added it to their two coffees on the counter.

She yawned again and got out her wallet to pay. After a brief exchange with the thankfully English-speaking clerk, they left the warm shop for the frigid walk to their rental car.

Jai frowned at her as he turned the key in the ignition and waited for the car to warm for a minute before throwing it into drive. "Why are you so tired? We turned in at like seven o'clock local time. You should have had plenty of rest."

"I didn't sleep well." She hoped Jai would leave it at that and not question her further as to why.

Not sleeping well was an understatement for last night's torture.

Emily had gotten back to her room after dinner and called Katie's office line to leave a message. She'd had to lie on the voicemail and tell Katie that everything with Hawk was going perfectly. That she could handle him no problem.

Then she'd fallen into bed, only to be tortured with more thoughts of Hawk as she relived each and every word exchanged between them.

That's probably what led to her dreaming about him. She hoped that was it anyway. Whatever the reason, dream she did.

It started with a photo shoot, which was understandable considering they'd had one that day. However, the model was BB and Katie was there. To her horror, Katie had begun to take BB's uniform off until he was nearly naked, then they'd started kissing each other as she watched.

Emily cringed even now at the thought. In her dream, she'd tried to look away but couldn't. Then something even more disturbing had happened. BB had morphed into Hawk, and the woman the mostly nude Hawk was making out with was suddenly no longer Katie, but Emily.

Her hands had been all over those big muscles of his as she stroked up and down his torso. It was so realistic she could feel the warmth of his skin, the hardness of his bulging biceps, the tickle of the hair on his chest against her palms. All while he'd made love to her mouth with his tongue.

She'd woken up totally freaked out and a little bit aroused. That had been it for sleep for the night.

With her brain spinning and her body clock messed up from the time difference, Emily had given up on bed and taken out her laptop.

Jai had downloaded the day's shots to her computer so she'd spent the rest of the time until she'd had to get ready to meet him working.

She'd taken Hawk's photos and played with the layout for some potential print ads.

Working with the pictures of him had done nothing to dispel the memories of that dream, but at least the work she'd done in the wee hours was a good non-sexual excuse to explain her lack of sleep to Jai.

"I woke up really early so I mocked up a few ads. I'll show them to you when we get there." She was happy to steer the discussion back to business.

"How do you think they look? Do you have all you'll need for the interior shots and close-ups?"

Emily had to admit she was pleased with what she'd had to work with and what she'd come up with.

Of course, telling Hawk he made a great model would

never come out of her mouth except maybe under extreme torture.

"I think so. Although, since he's so far away," *and such a pain in the ass,* "we might want to take some extras. And I never did get him into his dress uniform yesterday."

Or out of it, except in her dream.

"Mmm. Right. Make sure I'm in the room when you ask him to put on his dress outfit. That should be fun." Jai grinned.

Emily scowled. So much for her supposed ally.

CHAPTER ELEVEN

Hawk stood by the window and watched Goldilocks and Rasta-photographer park in front of the Head Shed and get out of their car.

Surrounding him, on nearly every available surface, was all the photographic equipment from the photo session he'd been forced to partake in yesterday.

Today, he'd have to do it all again, under the direction of the blonde who'd had him coming in his sleep like a teenaged boy.

He studied her more closely today than he had yesterday when he'd dismissed her as a young, silly, although cute, annoyance.

This morning, watching her juggle a large briefcase and an extra-large coffee cup as she walked down the path from the car, he realized his nocturnal imaginings had given her a slutty sort of makeover.

She didn't wear fuck-me high-heeled shoes or butt-bearing mini-skirts, and her nails weren't long, red talons at all.

Cocking his head to one side, he wondered why his brain would do that, because the blonde before him—nose pink from the cold, unruly curls tousled by the wind, all bundled up in her thick wool sweater and looking like the girl next door, was pretty damn cute in her own right.

He moved to the open doorway of the room, where he had a view of the main entrance of the building, just in time to see her push through the front door along with a burst of wind.

Goldilocks finally looked up and noticed him watching her.

"Morning." She met his gaze, mumbled the greeting and then looked away.

She made an obvious effort to not walk too closely to him as she passed by in the doorway. She seemed to be concentrating overly hard on setting her briefcase on one of the tables, all while not looking at him.

If Hawk weren't mistaken, she was avoiding eye contact as she set up her laptop.

Had he been such a beast yesterday that she couldn't even look at him today?

Thinking about it, he realized the answer was most likely yes, and that made him feel pretty shitty.

The new face of the Army, like it or not, and he was portraying himself as an ass. Probably not the best idea since performing even this bullshit assignment badly could negatively affect his chances at a promotion.

Smiling, Rasta-man was quite a bit more welcoming than Goldie. "Morning, Sergeant. Have you heard the weather forecast for today? All I could get on the television in the room was in German."

Predicting the weather here in winter was a no brainer. "Cold," Hawk answered.

Unwinding an incredibly long and multi-colored scarf from around his neck and dreadlocks, Rasta grinned. "Yeah, I'd gathered that already. But what about snow?"

The answer to that he had actually heard from one of the guys at chow. "No snow."

Rasta grinned. "Good. See, Em. Nothing to worry about." He turned toward Hawk. "City girl here reacts badly to snow."

Goldilocks, aka Em, glanced at her photographer as if she

wanted to take Rasta's scarf and strangle him with it.

"Will you be okay if we're outdoors today in this cold?" he continued, looking at Hawk.

Hawk raised a brow at Rasta's question, remembering his recent fun in the four-foot-deep drifts in the Alps. "Don't worry about me. You should probably worry about her though."

"I'll be fine, thank you." She raised one blonde brow and shot Hawk a less than friendly look, then turned back to her laptop screen. "Jai, can you take a look at the ad mock-ups so we know what more we need to get today?"

Very pointedly, she'd moved the subject away from herself and onto the job.

"You mean besides the dress . . . uniform?" Rasta-man laughed as he walked toward a pissed-looking Goldilocks.

Hawk's ears perked up, not about the dress uniform part, but about Goldie having the ads done already.

She moved fast. He'd assumed these frigging embarrassing photos wouldn't hit until well after next week when he was safely gone, but maybe he'd been wrong.

Trying to not look overly interested, Hawk used all of his vast skill and prowess learned over multiple tours of duty and sidled stealthily behind the two bent heads at the laptop.

Glancing past Rasta-man's dreadlocks, he caught a glimpse of a portion of an ad. His ad. That was his eye glaring back at him off the screen.

Damn, no wonder Goldie wouldn't look at him today. He did look kind of scary in that one.

Goldie turned in her seat, glimpsed his face and let out a frustrated huff of air. "You don't like it."

It hadn't sounded like a question, but rather a resignation-filled statement of fact.

"I didn't say that," Hawk defended.

"You didn't have to. You're frowning."

"No, I'm not." Hawk consciously smoothed his brow muscles.

Goldie turned back to the screen, but he thought he heard

a mumble sounding like, "Yeah, right."

With the click of her short, pale pink nails against the keyboard, the picture on screen changed to another one.

The two marketing gurus were discussing some fine points of demographics and target markets or something and didn't even notice him until Hawk readjusted his stance to try and see around them, which caught Rasta's attention.

"Hey, man. Sorry. I'm in your way. I'm sure you wanna see." After the other man moved aside, Hawk got his first full glimpse of himself.

He heard Goldie sigh. "I'm sure you hate this one too."

Hawk considered the photo before him on the screen for another second.

Legs planted wide, he stood wearing his T-shirt and camouflage pants with his arms crossed in front of his chest. His jaw set firm, there was no smile on his lips. His nose showed and part of his eye, but that was it. She'd cropped the photo so you couldn't see the rest of his face or even identify it as him.

He loved it.

Realizing he stood in that same pose now, Hawk had to admit, Goldie and Rasta had really captured his essence.

Hawk decided to throw Goldie a bone for her efforts. "I like it."

Visibly taken aback by the compliment, Goldie shook her head, as if she hadn't heard him correctly. "You like it?"

"Mmm, hmm. You cut off half of my face. Can't even tell it's me. I like it a lot."

Couldn't have her getting too cocky, now could he? At least Rasta-man seemed to appreciate Hawk's sense of humor. He broke out laughing while Goldie's face twisted into an angry frown.

"I agree. Not seeing your face is preferable. Perhaps I'll crop them all like that." Insult delivered, she spun back to the laptop.

"You do that, doll, and I'll owe you a big kiss plus some."

Goldie emitted something resembling a snort.

He smiled. She was sure fun to play with. In fact, reevaluating his former opinion of Goldie, Hawk decided he wouldn't mind at all playing with her some more. In all sorts of ways.

Still chuckling, Rasta moved across the room to fiddle with some of his camera equipment. "Em, I think we're good on indoor shots for now."

"What about the dress uniform ones?" Goldie shot Hawk a look. "Are you going to have any problems with us shooting you in your dress uniform?"

"As long as you don't use real bullets. No. No problem. Shoot away." Hawk smiled as she rolled her eyes at his corny joke.

He was pretty certain using real bullets had crossed her mind at one point that morning.

"Interior shots we can take anytime using the lights, Em. I'm anxious to get outdoors and scout some locations for the exterior shots while the weather is still good." Rasta-man glanced up from packing a bag full of stuff, most of which Hawk wouldn't have been able to identify the use of.

It wasn't his job to know photography equipment. It was his job to know his garrison.

Hawk really, really did not want to be helpful for this thing he was being forced to do. But against his will, his brain went into overdrive and he actually had an idea for the outdoor shoot. Rasta would love it and take a hundred more photos of him because of it, but Hawk knew he was going to share his idea anyway.

Though it had crossed his mind at one point to let them flounder on their own, he said, "I had some thoughts about the outdoor shots."

Looking amused, Goldie turned to him. "Really? You? Had thoughts?"

Hawk raised one brow and rose to the challenge. "Yeah, I do that occasionally. Think. Be real nice to me, Goldilocks, and I might share some of my more interesting thoughts with you sometime. I guarantee you'll enjoy it."

His pet name for her went over like a fart in church, judging by the expression on her face. He smiled again. Yeah, he definitely was enjoying this verbal foreplay. But time to get back to work so he could get this assignment over and done with.

"Anyway, I don't know what you're looking for exactly, if you want authentic-looking combat shots or not, but troops come to Hohenfels for realistic force-to-force combat maneuver training," Hawk began.

Rasta's eyes opened wide. "So you do mission rehearsals and stuff like that here?"

Hawk nodded. "Exactly."

"What do you use in the simulations? Lasers?"

Well, well. Rasta-man wasn't just a pretty face with a lot of hair. He had some sort of military experience, probably from behind the lens of his camera, but at least Hawk wouldn't have to explain everything to them both like children.

"We have a laser-engagement system and COBs—civilians on the battlefield—who help us train. There's a village set up, totally realistic, perimeter razerwire fencing, guard towers, MPs on patrol and civilian housing where the COBs live. You'd never know you weren't in Iraq or Afghanistan."

Rasta looked excited enough to jump right out of his coffee-colored skin at that description. "And we can get permission to shoot there?"

"Captain said whatever you wanted, he'd approve. Within reason," Hawk added.

Eyes wide, Rasta began grabbing his equipment faster and stowing it in bags. "Great. Let's go."

Goldie watched him. "I guess it's all set then."

Hawk grinned. So she didn't like not being in control. Interesting and something to remember for the future.

Rasta paused and glanced at her. "Sorry, Em. Did you have an idea for something else?"

"No. I think we should trust Hawk's experience."

Goldilocks was going to trust him. He liked that idea.

Today was turning out to be pretty interesting all around.

CHAPTER TWELVE

In the dimly lit comfort of her hotel room, Emily stared into the haunting eyes of Staff Sergeant David *Hawk* Hawkins and realized her heart was not only beating faster, but parts lower were beginning to throb as well.

She reached out one finger. Running it down the screen along the side of his cheek, she shook her head at her own behavior.

Darn it. What was wrong with her libido? She should not be attracted to him. He was an unpredictable idiot.

Hawk acted like a total jerk one moment, but then he came up with the perfect suggestion for their shoot the next. He'd even cooperated during it.

She'd seen a different side of him today when he'd taken her and Jai for a tour of the outdoor training village. Then more of that strange new side of him when, familiar, alert, capable, he'd posed for shots with huge, scary weapons like they were an extension of his body.

It was a glimpse into what he must be like when he was with his men being a professional soldier instead of being a pain in her ass as a model.

The man was gorgeous to look at on the outside, and a cocky, male chauvinistic pig on the inside. And she had to admit she wanted him.

Emily leaned back from the laptop screen and the photo of Hawk decked out in his dress uniform. His chest was covered in ribbons or medals or whatever they were called. His face was stern as usual, his chin firm, his eyes piercing straight through her.

There might be more inside this man than she'd seen. Of course, that something more could be either good or bad. There was no telling for sure, but she would never know. She left for New York tomorrow.

Emily let out a sigh. She and Jai had tickets on a late-morning flight out of Germany. She was returning to work and to her boss a success with enough photos for a kick-butt ad campaign. She was also returning home without the Prince Charming she'd been so sure of finding.

A knock on the door made Emily jump nearly out of her desk chair.

"Em. You still awake in there?" Jai's voice followed the knock.

Happy she hadn't taken the time to change into her flannel pajamas, knowing Jai would tease her relentlessly for certain if she had, Emily opened the door for him.

"No, I'm not asleep. And if I had been, you sure would have woken me up."

He grinned. "But you weren't sleeping, so it's all good. And since you're awake . . . there's a Ratskeller on this block. What do you say we go out and sample some of the local culture in the form of German beer and nightlife for our last night here?"

"I don't know. I thought I'd work on some more print ad mock-ups —"

"You can do that tomorrow during the flight while I sleep off a nice dark-lager hangover."

Emily laughed. No doubt that would be exactly how the flight would go.

"Okay." Then she glanced down at her wool trousers and sweater, the same ones she'd worn all day. "Am I dressed all right for a Ratskeller? I don't think I've ever been to one."

"Em, it's just a bar. You're overdressed, I'm sure. Just come on."

She'd have to trust Jai's fashion advice. She had no other choice. The rest of her wardrobe already packed in her luggage looked pretty much like what she had on but in a different color.

Emily grabbed her wallet out of her briefcase and her room key and headed out.

The minute she walked into the bar she felt it, eyes on her. Lots of them, all male, and judging by the fact Hawk stood in the center of the group of males watching her, she guessed they were all soldiers from the neighboring garrison.

They weren't in uniform, but they did all sport the signature military cropped hair. Two of them even walked in sync when they crossed the bar to the jukebox together.

Hawk smiled and crossed the room himself, but he wasn't following the other two. He was heading right for her. Emily took a deep breath and prepared for another verbal battle.

"Good evening, Sergeant," Jai greeted Hawk.

Hawk nodded a return greeting to Jai then he turned to her. "Hey, Goldilocks. Fancy seeing you here."

Her brows shot up, but that was all the reaction she allowed him. "Sergeant Hawkins."

Jae grinned, apparently amused at her new name. At least it was her name as far as Hawk was concerned. "Em. I'm going to get us two beers. Good with you?"

"Yeah, fine. Thanks." She scowled at her supposed friend for enjoying Hawk's teasing of her so much, but accepted his offer.

Glancing back at Hawk, she had a feeling a beer, or three, would be in order tonight.

As Jai left them alone, she raised her chin.

"Do you even know my name?" She confronted Hawk as he towered over her.

He grinned wider. "Yeah."

"Okay. Then what is it?" Emily crossed her arms and challenged him over the noise of the many bar patrons.

Leaning down, Hawk came so close she could feel his breath brush her ear. "It's Emily, Goldilocks."

She shivered involuntarily at the feel of his warm breath against her skin and swallowed hard, unsure what to say.

It was a simple answer to her question, though delivered in a far more intimate manner than she'd expected. She certainly never expected it to affect her as it had.

Deciding the safest course of action would be to change the subject, she did just that. "So, I looked over the shots from today. They look really great. I could email you the proofs if you wanted to see them."

Then she would have not only his email address, but also an excuse to be in contact with him after she left Germany tomorrow. Why did her heart race at that idea?

He was a jerk, most of the time anyway. Like now as he shrugged. "Whatever."

"Don't you care about the ads?"

"I have to tell you, doll. I won't waste one moment thinking about this modeling thing once the rounds start flying and the baddies start to fall."

"Fine, I won't bother you with them then."

Looking actually sincere, Hawk shook his head. "I didn't say you'd be bothering me. What I meant was I'll have a few things on my mind, like bringing the men depending on me home alive. Latest word from where we'll be in the Afghan mountains is that a storm dumped a few feet of snow and more will be on its way. And that's the good news, because at least with the snow mounds building up we actually have a perimeter defense."

"Oh." Emily didn't know much about perimeter defense, but she did hate the snow and could empathize with him about that. "Hopefully they'll get the snowplows to clean all that up before you guys get there."

Hawk laughed—a deep, rich, genuine belly laugh she'd never assumed he was capable of.

Emily frowned. "What?"

Why was this guy always laughing at her expense?

Hawk could barely respond through his laughter. "Oh, Goldilocks. There aren't going to be road crews cleaning up for us."

"Isn't where you're going kind of like the set up here at Hohenfels?"

Hawk tilted his head to one side and grinned. "No, it's not."

"Oh. I figured all bases were probably the same." Emily shrugged. What did she know? It was pretty rude of him to think she should.

"No, doll. They're not, but I'm not going to a base anyway." He smiled, shaking his head. "If I was going to be at Kandahar or Bagram, then yeah, maybe we'd have some services, but not where I'll be. We literally have some dirt huts and a few rail boxes. Supplies will have to be choppered in and dropped to us. It'll be like going caveman."

Not appreciating his delight at her expense, Emily grumbled, "That should be easier for some of you than others, I suppose."

He raised one dark brow with amusement. "You calling me a caveman, doll?"

"Maybe." Emily smiled, enjoying her own cleverness.

It was the strangest thing, but bickering with Hawk kind of got her excited. Even his calling her *doll* was starting to sound sexy, and she hadn't even drunk the beer that Jai was now carrying her way.

Hawk, looking like he got as much pleasure from the sparring as she did, grinned wide as Jai joined them.

"Sergeant, did Emily tell you? The shots we took at the training village today are awesome."

"Good, I'm glad." Strangely, Hawk looked like he meant it.

Emily grasped the topic of work before she gave in to imagining running her fingers down Hawk's massive forearm, and other things.

"I agree with Jai. The SpecOps ads Katie shot with BB were all taken in a studio. They were good but nothing like ours. The ones we took outdoors today look really authentic, like we actually shot in the war zone. As great as BB was, I think our Army ads will be even more effective because they look so real. Right down to our caveman model, here." Emily grinned and sipped her beer.

Hawk raised his glass in a salute. "Thanks. I think that might be the nicest thing you've ever said to me."

Emily laughed. "You're welcome."

"Fucking Dalton." Hawk shook his head and took another swallow from his own glass.

That got Emily's defenses up. He could pick on her, but no one picked on her boss's fiancé in front of her. "What's wrong with BB? He's practically perfect."

Hawk laughed. "If he's your perfect man, sweet thing, then I don't know what the hell you're doing hanging around with me."

Annoyed with him all over again, she stood a little straighter, but he still towered over her. "I'm not hanging around with you. You're hanging around with me. Jai and I came here tonight to absorb some local color before we leave tomorrow morning."

Jai glanced from her to Hawk and back again with a strange expression on his face. "Um, I see Sergeant Pettit over there. I think I'll go ask him . . . something."

Hawk grabbed Jai's arm. "Pettit knows the truth about all this, and he also knows I'll kill him if he spills the beans. But as far as the rest of them know—" he bobbed his head in the direction of the soldiers across the room standing with Pettit, "—you and she were here for the last two days taking photos of the garrison, not of me. Let's keep it that way, understood? As far as my squad is concerned, my assignment was to be your escort only. That's all. Got it?"

Jai laughed and shook his head. "Yeah, I got it. Don't worry, Sergeant."

Hawk looked more than a bit concerned as he watched Jai cross the room.

"He'll keep your secret," Emily assured him, thinking all

the secrecy was stupid since his face would soon be in ads pretty much everywhere.

Hawk continued to track Jai as he joined the group of soldiers. "How long have you known him?"

"Jai? A few years, I guess. He's discreet, I promise."

He raised a brow. "You two fucking?"

"What? No." She nearly choked at the question. God, he could be so crude sometimes. "You are the rudest, biggest, nosiest . . ."

Unable to figure out how to insult him more, she left the sentence open ended.

"And you hate it that you find me attractive." He treated her to a crooked grin before sipping his beer.

"You? Attractive? Ha!" That accusation had her sputtering. Okay, maybe she did think he was hot, but he didn't have to know that. "Don't flatter yourself. You're a job. Nothing more."

"Keep telling yourself that, Goldie. Maybe you'll start believing it. Although, I find that alcohol usually has the opposite effect on a woman's libido."

Hawk smirked and glanced at the beer in her hand, which she had been steadily emptying during their sparring without even realizing it. She'd nearly finished it, and it was starting to affect her head but not her wit.

"I see. So what you're saying is girls need to be drunk to find you attractive. That's totally understandable." Emily smirked right back.

Hawk shook his head. "You are cute when you try and fight with me. The question is why are you fighting this so hard, doll? I know you're attracted to me. You know you're attracted to me. You're leaving tomorrow. I'm leaving in about a week." He let the facts hang in the air for her to absorb and draw her own conclusions.

"Are you saying we should . . ." She could barely get the words out past the tightness his unspoken suggestion had caused in her throat.

"Have sex? Yup, I sure am." He grinned.

Could she do it? Did she want to? Have sex just for fun with a man she barely knew?

Although she did know him, didn't she? They'd spent two days together. She knew some of his personal and probably all of his military history from his file. She knew that for some reason, BB had chosen this man to represent the entire US Army. She could see that both Hawk's superiors and his subordinates liked him. All of that had to count for something.

"You sure are doing a lot of thinking in there, Goldie." Hawk ran one thick finger from her forehead, between her drawn brows and down her nose, tapping the tip playfully. "Stop frowning. You'll get wrinkles."

Emily fought the shiver that his touch sent down her spine and decided it wouldn't hurt to play along, for a bit anyway. "Let's say, under the influence of some sort of temporary insanity and German beer, that I did consider sleeping with you—"

"Oh, believe me, there'd be no sleeping. Just good old-fashioned sex. Incredible, unforgettable sex. Lots of it."

Emily swallowed hard. She didn't know if she'd ever experienced sex that qualified as that before. Certainly not in recent memory. She forced herself to focus on her point again.

"Anyway. If this were to happen, hypothetically of course, what would it mean?"

"What would it mean?" Hawk repeated.

"Yes, what would it mean?"

He laughed. "It would mean that you and I would both walk away satisfied. Me to Afghanistan. You to wherever you come from. It would mean that you would never have to deal with me and my brutish caveman ways again. However, you would have some damn nice memories to keep you warm at night. As would I, and believe me, a year in Afghanistan with no sex, I'm going to need the memories."

"A year? Really?" Okay, so she'd gone a good year herself without sex, but Hawk didn't seem like the type to be celibate by choice.

"Doll, even if sex while deployed weren't against regulations, there aren't going to be any females where I'll be. Just those ten ugly mugs over there, and I don't go that way." Hawk glanced at his fellow soldiers and shook his head.

"So I could possibly be the last woman you were with? For a year?" Somehow knowing she could be the last woman he'd be with before going off to risk his life in the war got her feeling all tingly. Patriotic even.

Sex for the good of the country. Supporting the troops took on a whole new meaning.

"Mmm hmm, and not just possibly. Most definitely. Tonight is our last hurrah. There won't be any time with getting ready to deploy to go out for beer or women. You're it, doll." He smiled and ran his hand up her arm. It sent a chill through her in spite of the hot, stale air in the bar. "The last woman I'll touch for an entire long, lonely year. The one I'll picture at night when I'm all alone in my cold, dark bunk."

Emily drew in a shaky breath. Her body wanted this man, and now her brain, which was usually the rational of the two, was starting to think it was a good idea too.

Hawk stepped closer. "Come on, doll. Do something just for the fun of it once in your life. Go tell your friend over there that you're tired and going back to your room."

She glanced at the group of soldiers surrounding Jai. "Even if I leave alone and you sneak upstairs later, they'll notice when you leave too. They'll all know."

"My men? Maybe. Probably. So what if they know? Do you really care? You'll never see any of them again, and they'll all be envying me spending one of our last nights in civilization with the prettiest girl in this place."

Damn, he was good. The caveman didn't talk often, but when he decided to, it was good stuff. She was really going to do this.

She took her last swallow of beer to bolster her nerves. "Room two-ten at the hotel next door. Please try to be as discreet as you can so they don't know."

He looked about as surprised at her decision as she was herself. She'd shocked him.

Emily took note of that with a smile, then turned to go lie to Jai. He'd most likely see right through her, but she had to make the attempt.

The worst part was that what Hawk had said was true. At the moment, with her heart pounding and her body throbbing, she couldn't really care what anyone thought about her tomorrow. She was only concerned with tonight.

CHAPTER THIRTEEN

Room two-ten. Hawk swallowed hard and stared at the brass numbers on the door while the condoms purchased from the men's room at the Ratskeller felt heavy in his jeans pocket.

Once within the inner sanctum, Hawk's plan was to avoid talking at all costs. Emily was most likely the kind of woman who scared off easily. The last thing he wanted was to say something wrong and her to change her mind.

He couldn't risk Emily turning tail and running. Not when he was this close. One thing Hawk knew for sure when it came to women, he never assumed he was in until he was, well, *in*.

Emily. Funny how now that he stood outside her hotel room, feet from her, moments from making last night's erotic dream come true, he didn't think of her as Goldilocks anymore.

That was quite a change. Usually the women he slept with remained forever Red or Blondie or Legs or whatever name he'd dubbed them at first sight.

Maybe the difference was he and Emily had a professional relationship too. Who the hell knew? Nothing about this girl and his attraction to her made sense.

She wasn't his usual type. Hell, she was pretty much the exact opposite of it.

They fought like cats and dogs, and at times he was fairly sure she outright hated him. Yet here he was, outside her hotel room and at her invitation no less. Maybe the fighting was what made them so hot for each other.

Hawk realized he was wasting time on the wrong side of the door with all this thinking.

Thinking. About a woman. That was also totally unlike him.

He raised a fist and knocked loudly, holding his breath that she'd answer.

Answer she did. The door opened and Emily, still in the clothes she'd worn to the bar, stepped back to allow Hawk to enter. He took a step forward into the room and suddenly had an arm full of woman.

Good thing he had fast reflexes. He caught her and managed to not fall backward onto his ass as she dove at him. Wrapping her legs around his waist, she crashed her lips into his.

Hawk shouldered the door shut with the hope it would lock on its own. Angling his head to take full advantage of her hungry kiss, he didn't give the damn door another thought as Emily's tongue invaded his mouth.

Figuring they would end up there anyway, he stepped heavily toward the bed with Emily wrapped around his neck and waist.

A willing woman literally in his hands was good, but one in the bed was even better. There he'd be free to unwrap the wool-covered package and enjoy what was underneath.

More than that, holding her up was severely limiting his participation in this unexpectedly enthusiastic but more than welcome foreplay she'd initiated.

Hawk prided himself on the prowess of both his hands and mouth, and he intended to show off all his skills for this woman. They may have only one night together, but as he set

88

her down and braced above her, he vowed he would make sure she never forgot it.

Beneath him on the mattress, Emily squirmed and broke their kiss. He raised himself up on shaky arms, afraid he had crushed her with his not-inconsiderable weight.

He needn't have worried.

All he could do was groan in response when one of her hands pulled at the turtleneck tucked into his jeans while the other fumbled with his fly.

"Clothes off." She'd said only two breathless words.

Two words were enough, and he couldn't agree more. He wanted them skin-to-skin.

Since she was obviously willing, who was he to slow them down?

He'd get them both naked, but right now he craved her mouth again.

With a long, low growl, he held her head and dove in for one more quick taste of her warm and inviting lips.

Untangling his hand from the mass of her hair, he set to work on getting them undressed as fast as possible. She helped, and by the time his clothes were in a heap on the floor so were hers.

Then Hawk really had something to groan about. Her bulky sweater had hid more than just her soft, ivory skin. It also had disguised two perfectly shaped peaks tipped with rosy nipples.

"Damn, you're beautiful." To Hawk's surprise that was no bullshit. He meant every word.

"You're not so bad yourself," she whispered while she explored his now-bare chest with her hands.

From the top of her blonde head to the tips of her pale-pink polished toes, and everything in between, this woman was a man's wet dream.

Better than Hawk's latest dream actually, because she was real, in more ways than one. All of her. Every last inch was God-given temptation.

He'd always been a boob man, usually the bigger the better. But after a run of chicks with plastic parts, everything from breast implants to surgically plumped lips, Emily's natural perfection was a huge turn-on.

Hawk ran his tongue over one tightly pebbled nipple and watched her shiver. He liked that reaction, a lot, so he took the bite-sized tidbit into his mouth and sucked hard.

She groaned and lifted her spine off the bed to press farther into his mouth.

Damn. If the rest of her was equally as sensitive, they were both in for one hell of a wild ride. He could hardly wait.

When Emily spread her legs to give him room to lie between them, he didn't hesitate.

Heart pounding, Hawk nestled his throbbing erection against her folds.

Hard enough to drive nails with the thing, he nudged a bit and found her slick and ready. "You're so wet."

"I've been that way for two days now." Her voice came out sounding raspy.

They'd first met two days ago. She was finally admitting she'd wanted him from the very beginning. That knowledge was nearly his undoing.

Hawk held himself very still as he tried to resist plunging unprotected into her. The way he felt, he didn't trust himself to not lose it the minute he was inside this woman.

The dead-last thing he needed was a little David Hawkins Junior running around back in the States while he was in Afghanistan chasing baddies through the mountains.

At the speed of light, Hawk grabbed the packet from the pocket of his jeans and covered himself.

He slid deep inside Emily with one sure stroke.

Throwing her head back against the pillow, she groaned as he pushed inside.

He'd never expected her to react so readily to his each and every touch. He was thrilled. And surprised. He should have known it was the ones you least expected it from who were the hottest in bed.

As he pulled out then slid back inside, Emily grabbed his hips and raised her own. Her eyes opened and he became caught in her blue gaze.

It took him a second to realize he'd stopped all movement as he got lost in the depths of her heavily lidded eyes.

Shaking himself out of it, he reached down to raise her ass higher off the bed, then set a fast, hard pace.

She was gasping in moments, her body clenching at his. He moved faster as her cries grew louder, until he felt her shatter around him.

He couldn't help but watch her face as she came. So beautiful.

The woman always in control had lost control and it was his doing. Both his ego and his cock swelled at the thought until a feeling touched his heart. Regret maybe?

He wanted more of her than just this night.

Wanting what he couldn't have, especially on the eve of leaving for war, was a bad thing.

While she still gasped for breath and the aftershocks of her climax still gripped him, he pulled out. He flipped a boneless Emily over so she lay face down on the bed and he couldn't see those eyes that would surely haunt his dreams for the next year.

While her cries were muffled by the pillow, he plunged inside her. Hard and fast, over and over, he tried to lose himself in the act, rather than the woman.

As her body met his thrust for thrust, he pounded himself to completion.

Hawk collapsed over Emily's heaving back.

His head landed on the pillow next to hers and she angled her face toward his.

The sounds of her breath filled his ear, the softness of her hair pillowed his cheek, her scent engulfed him and he knew, for better or worse, he'd never forget any of it.

CHAPTER FOURTEEN

The man slept like the dead.

No sooner had he shuddered inside her, left to flush the condom and then slipped back between the covers, he was out like a light.

Not a word. Just silence, then unconsciousness.

She'd felt him literally fall into sleep. The rock-like muscle-bound arm he'd thrown over her had gotten heavier and heavier, pinning her in place at his side.

Not that she blamed him for being physically worn out. He had expended quite a bit of energy.

It wasn't like he'd left her unsatisfied and wanting or anything. No, she'd done quite a bit of shuddering herself. But still, how could he fall asleep so fast and so soundly?

His even breathing told her he certainly wasn't spending any time on second thoughts about what had happened between them.

Emily glanced at the clock. She'd been second guessing herself and what had happened for an hour and a half now.

On top of not being able to sleep, she had to pee.

Back in New York, counting the days until she met her supposed Prince Charming, Emily had imagined a similar scenario. Snuggling in bed after making love, bodies intertwined, falling asleep in his arms feeling warm, safe and loved.

Nowhere in her visions had it been a one-night stand, and in her dreams she hadn't had to desperately use the bathroom.

Waiting any longer was not an option. It would just be too bad if she woke Sleeping Beauty.

Emily wiggled her way free of the vise that was Hawk's arm and slipped from the bed. When she returned from the bathroom, she found he hadn't moved a muscle.

Some war-hardened, trained fighter he was. She could probably set off a bomb under the bed and he wouldn't wake up.

"Sure hope the Taliban doesn't sneak up on you at night or you're a goner," she whispered and crawled back under the warm covers with a shiver.

"I heard that." Hawk readjusted his position to accommodate her reentry to the bed. With her back against his front, he flung his arm over her waist.

"Well, it's true. You sleep like a rock."

"Yeah. When I know it's safe. Otherwise the slightest sound—a boot crunching, someone breathing too loud—it'll all wake me up. Believe me."

"Oh."

What else could she say about that? She knew nothing about what this man went through on a daily basis and she probably never would. Another reason her decision to jump him, literally, and hop right into bed was probably ill advised.

Mistake or not, as long as she'd done it once, she might as well do it again. If he was up for it.

Emily wiggled back against him. "Speaking of sleeping, what was all that talk in the bar about how there'd be no sleeping tonight? Hmm?"

"I have an excuse. You wore me out. I didn't know Goldilocks would turn into the Big Bad Wolf in bed." Two big arms gathered her up and pulled her closer to his chest.

As he kissed up and down her neck and shoulder she felt him grow hard against her naked butt.

"You're mixing your fairytales." Emily sighed as the physical sensations sweeping through her from his touch battled with her emotions.

She'd been more forward with Hawk than she'd ever been with any other man in her past, as few of them as there'd been.

What he must think of her after that. She hated to even consider it.

"What's bothering you, doll? I can feel you frowning from here."

"I'm wondering how stupid sleeping with you was. I don't usually do this, you know." It wasn't exactly easy to think with his naked body pressed against her, making her warm inside and out, but she managed to answer the question.

"Do what? Have incredible sex with irresistible soldiers you've only known for two days?"

"Yes. The two-day part, at least. The irresistible part is pushing it, don't you think?" Sparring with Hawk brought Emily back into her comfort zone.

He chuckled against her back. "You still don't like the idea that you wanted me from the minute you walked into that office, do you?"

Actually, it was from the minute his eyes had stared back at her from the computer printout back in New York, but she wasn't telling him that. And because of that instant attraction, she should have run from the Ratskeller the moment she realized Hawk was inside.

She'd fallen half in love with Hawk before ever meeting him, imagining a fairytale happy ever after with her Army prince.

Even the reality of two days of fighting with him over every detail of this campaign hadn't squelched that attraction. So what had she gone and done? She jumped into bed with him, willing to settle for one night over nothing at all.

Stupid, stupid, stupid.

"You're doing it again." His voice was low and deep.

"Doing what?"

"Thinking."

He was right. She was thinking, because having sex with Hawk brought up a good dozen or so questions.

Would she ever hear from him again? If she did have to contact him again for work, how weird would it be? What if he got injured or killed? Or what if he was just fine but she still never heard from him again?

"I can't help it." Emily sighed.

"Well, I can." He skimmed his hand from her waist to her hip, and then down to her thigh. There, he paused and made small circles against her skin.

"You can what? Not think? Yeah, I figured that."

"No, my witty little thinker. I meant I can stop you from thinking."

His large, rough hand pulled her leg up and over his hip. With her spread wide, he found her most sensitive spot and began stroking. Her eyes closed involuntarily as he worked her.

The tension began to build and she breathlessly shuddered out a moan.

"Still thinking?" He nipped at her neck after delivering that question against her ear.

"Shut up, Hawk." With her body coiling, tensing for release, her rapid breathing should have given him his answer.

Hawk chuckled just as the hip-bucking orgasm broke over her.

She was still quivering when he covered himself with a condom and slid inside her. Then Hawk wasn't laughing any longer.

There was no joking, no more talking at all, as he set a fast pace.

After a few incredibly wonderful minutes of him thrusting into her, his grip tightened on her hips. With a deep groan that reverberated straight through her body, he came. She felt him throb inside her.

He laid his head against hers, breathing hard behind her. "Damn. I could happily do that again right now, but we both need a shower first. I've got some tasty plans for more fun and I want us both extra clean for it."

Emily groaned in protest, not at the idea of more sex, but that it meant getting out of the warm bed again. Germans needed to turn up the thermostats in their hotels. Keeping a room this cold was barbaric.

"Now? It's cold out there."

"Yes, now. And don't you worry about being cold. I'll warm you up. Trust me." He grabbed her hand and pulled her up and out of the blessed warmth of the sheets.

Emily glanced down and took in his spectacularly naked, beautifully muscular form. The thick thighs, small waist and indescribably large forearms.

She imagined him bracing her against the wall of the shower stall as he plunged inside her.

Oh boy.

Just the mere thought of sex with Hawk again had her heart racing, and they'd just finished. It couldn't be good to want a man this much, especially when she'd probably never see him again.

"Are you sure you don't want to go back to sleep? You seemed pretty tired before." Nerves had Emily resorting to teasing him.

Well on the way to being hard again, Hawk took a step closer until their bodies touched. "I think we're done sleeping for the night. What do you think?"

Not having even closed her eyes yet, forget about getting any sleep, Emily still nodded in agreement.

She had only one night with this man. She would make the most of it and deal with the consequences later.

CHAPTER FIFTEEN

Afghanistan—the most heavily mined place in the world—and for better or worse, Hawk's home for the next year. He got his first glimpse of the desolate region in the dim light of dusk.

The plane carrying him, his squad and their loaded pallet of gear landed without incident at the old Kandahar International Airport, now being used as the base airfield.

Having secured a seat in the front row of the C14 aircraft, Hawk's boots hit the ground ahead of his men as he took his first step onto Afghan soil.

The blast of frigid air in his face served as the local welcoming committee. The base was at a high altitude and there were mountains off in the distance everywhere he looked.

Kandahar was only the initial stop on their tour of Afghanistan. Next up, Bagram Air Base, then a quick hop on a helicopter to their final destination, the mountainous outskirts of Kabul, where the insurgents waited for them. He had no doubt he'd make the baddies regret his squad's arrival.

Hawk and his men had gotten their official Afghan primer back at Hohenfels, but during their quick welcome tour of the base at Kandahar, he realized that actually being here, seeing the sights, listening to the stories and first-hand experiences of the Army guys who'd already been there, was quite an eye opener.

The base was riddled with crashed Russian helicopters from the war in the eighties. Even the rafters for the roof of one of the buildings was made from old Russian helicopter blades.

Yup, there were some very cool things about Kandahar—but Hawk was beginning to reevaluate that opinion as he sat in the dining hall during chow and got an earful from one of the guys stationed there.

"When they talk about landmines, they ain't shitting you. There are old landmines everywhere outside the fence." The soldier from the 10th Mountain Division dropped that information before casually scooping up some potatoes.

Landmines. That was enough to make Hawk lose his appetite for the boiled carrots, mashed potatoes and ketchup-covered meatloaf littering his plate. But since he had no intention of venturing outside the fence during his brief stopover, it shouldn't be an issue—for here and for today at least.

Who knew what surprises the region he was heading to held?

"So there are a bunch of Canadian troops here, huh?" Wally talked right through a mouthful of macerated meat.

Across the table, their welcoming party of one nodded. "Yup. But there are a lot of US Army units too. The main ground force is from the 10th Mountain like me. The Army aviation units attached to us are from all over. There's reserve units on base as well."

"I was told to expect a ton of snow where we're heading." Unlike Wally, Pettit asked his question *before* he shoved another forkful of food into his mouth.

The soldier let out a snort. "Snow? Yeah, there's snow, and cold, but that's nothing compared to what it's like here in the summer."

Wally took one glance at the expression of concern on Pettit's face and laughed. "I'm from Alabama. I can handle the heat."

The soldier shook his head. "The heat's not the issue. Don't get me wrong, it's hot, but the real problem's the sand. It's baby-powder fine and boy, does it blow. There are sandstorms all the time in summer. Damn stuff gets into everything. Feels like I'm always cleaning it out of my damn weapon."

Four-foot snowstorms that hit overnight in winter and sandstorms every day in summer. Lovely.

Hawk never thought he'd find a place that made Iraq look appealing, but here in Afghanistan he may have done just that. Thank you, Uncle Sam for the all-expenses-paid year-long vacation in Hell.

"Don't worry too much about the weather though. It's the locals you really need to watch out for."

As the soldier kept talking, what he said had Hawk laying down his fork and knife so he could give the unbelievable tale his full attention.

Wally's eyes opened wide. "I've heard rumors about the locals doing some sick shit, like hiding IEDs in corpses so when the soldiers go to investigate the body they get blown to kingdom come."

"That's no rumor. It's fact. Some of the locals are crazy bastards. We pay off the warlords to allow our convoys to drive back and forth to our forward operating base. A few years back a warlord, who was on our side because we paid him to be, skinned a local alive for attacking American soldiers. He hung his body on a post for everyone to see as an example."

Hawk shook his head in horrified disbelief. "Shit."

"Jesus." Pettit hissed under his breath.

"I know. It's the stuff of movies, but it's real. Hey, you can see the house and compound belonging to one of the warlords from the fences at the airfield. Ask someone to point it out to you when you leave."

All just part of the Kandahar sightseeing tour Hawk supposed. He let out a sigh as he wondered exactly what the chances were he and all his guys would get out of Afghanistan alive.

A year from now, how many would be coming back through Kandahar on the journey home with all their parts in working order?

He'd thought more than a few times about what he'd like to do with sweet little Emily when he finally got home next year, and then he'd thought better of it. Now, hearing the horror stories, he was even more certain. His decision to avoid anything more with her was the correct choice.

Hawk didn't need the image of Emily crying for him back home distracting him downrange.

She was probably pissed as hell at him. When she'd emailed him the photos from the shoot, he emailed back, but only once and he'd kept it short.

It was for the best. In the end, she would thank him . . . if he were around to be thanked.

Having a relationship while deployed was too hard for both parties involved. Hawk needed one hundred and ten percent of his attention on the job. Not on her.

If she was still available, and if he was still alive, he'd deal with her anger when he got back Stateside.

The vision of tempering an angry Emily put a smile on his face.

Hawk tucked that little scenario away to enjoy later when he was in the semi-privacy of their temporary lodging for the night. But right now, he needed to arm himself with as much info as he could to make sure he got himself and his men home.

He turned his attention back to the soldier across from him. "What else have you heard about what's waiting for us in those mountains in the Kabul Province? Whatever you can tell me, I wanna hear. All of it."

CHAPTER SIXTEEN

Emily walked into the meeting late, which was not her fault at all.

Someone had fallen onto the subway tracks, so they'd stopped service to rescue the idiot. She felt justified in calling the person an idiot because they weren't hurt and really, who leans so far over the tracks to see if the train is coming that they actually fall in unless they are brain dead?

Anyway, her train had been late. Consequently, so was she for a meeting with Katie and the big bosses—the owners of the agency—aka the guys who signed her paycheck. These guys were important.

She was sticking with blaming the subway. Emily tried not to think about how she had already been running late that morning after having slept like crap the night before because she was once again reliving her one night with Hawk.

Her brain knew thinking about him was pointless. It should anyway, she told it enough. Yet the rebellious gray matter continued to disobey common sense the minute the lights went out at night. She had no control over it.

She burst into the meeting room and interrupted the conversation in progress.

"Sorry." Cringing, she flung her bulging laptop bag on the conference table while at the same time offering that hurried apology.

Mr. Howard, as in the Howard & Dean Agency, nodded in her direction but didn't say anything about it. Hopefully that was a good thing, Emily wasn't sure.

Apparently, Emily looked as flustered as she felt. Katie smiled sympathetically and said loud enough for everyone to hear, "Tough ride in?"

Thank goodness for Katie, smoothing things over.

Emily answered with a short laugh. "They stopped the subway for somebody on the tracks, but I'm here now. Ready to get to it."

"You're just in time." Mr. Dean, the other half of the partnership, resumed the meeting. "We were about to review preliminary results of the Army campaign. The client reports they've tracked a small spike in recruitment since the new Army ads hit. However—"

Uh, oh. Howevers were never good.

"—it's not nearly as large a response as the SpecOps ads yielded last year. We need to evaluate why that is. Any ideas, people?" Mr. Dean glanced at the employees assembled expectantly.

Katie shrugged. "I'd have to say that I'm not sure we can expect the same level of response. It's apples and oranges trying to compare SpecOps and enlisted Army. We portrayed SpecOps as elite, which made people want it more."

Mr. Howard nodded. "That's exactly why we didn't take the same approach to the Army campaign. Our goal, which was successful in some respects and not so in others, is to show the Army soldier as a warrior, a protector of our freedom, yet at the same time, make it so that young men and woman can identify with him. Relate to him. See themselves in his shoes . . . or rather combat boots. Todd, the ad please."

Mr. Howard's assistant, Todd, instantly held up one of the print ads.

Suddenly Hawk's piercing eyes bore directly into Emily as she stared at the glossy photograph before her. Her traitorous heart began beating faster.

The perfect tag-team player, Mr. Dean took over where his partner had left off. "Take a look at this ad. Our man has the terrifying-warrior look down pat. The question is how do we make him appear more accessible to the average man and woman?"

Katie sat up straighter in her chair and pushed aside the ever-present box of crackers she ate to combat the morning sickness. She kept it next to her at all times now since she'd decided to reveal her pregnancy to the entire company.

"Perhaps that's the difference in the response. Accessibility. BB did a press tour as the SpecOps ads hit. National television appearances on the morning talk shows, local radio stations in targeted areas, live appearances. We're also missing the advantage of being connected to a big name. Remember, we piggy-backed the recruitment ads on top of a national Andre Milano underwear campaign starring BB, already a familiar name."

Howard and Dean nodded as one.

Emily nearly choked. Hawk was unhappy about posing for her in his uniform. She shuddered to think how he would react if they decided he had to pose in designer underwear.

And she cringed at even the thought of having to tell Hawk he was going to be interviewed by the five chattering ladies of *The View*, like BB had so willingly been.

She had to put a stop to this and now.

Emily raised her hand to speak. She was used to being the assistant, sitting silently, taking notes, supplying what Katie needed just like Mr. Howard's assistant, Todd, and Mr. Dean's assistant, Marci. She wasn't used to being an active participant, but as this was her assignment, she had to speak up.

Mr. Dean noted her raised hand and bobbed his head in her direction with an amused smile. "Emily?"

"Hawk, um, Staff Sergeant Hawkins, the model, is currently deployed in Afghanistan. We would have to get the approval of his commanders to have him sent home for that kind of press tour." Nervous, Emily spoke quickly, hoping all the while that the words *I had sex with the model* weren't emblazoned in her expression and tone.

"I don't think there's a need to have him sent back here." Mr. Howard shook his head. "Afghanistan is perfect. Do the tour over there."

Emily could almost see the wheels of his mind turning as the idea formed.

She frowned. "But there's a war on. I have no idea how we'd get a United States soldier booked on the *Good Day, Afghanistan* show or whatever."

Her little joke earned her a frown from Mr. Howard. "I don't expect you to. We need to show this soldier in his element, not sitting around drinking coffee and chatting with some show's hostess. I want him eating with his men, working out at the base gym, training. Or, you know, a video of him handing out dolls or chocolate or whatever to the little Afghan kiddies."

Mr. Dean nodded, looking excited about the idea. "That would cover the other aspect of this campaign. The client wants the market to realize the Army's focus is the people over there. Giving the war a face the public can relate to is just as important as giving the Army a relatable personality. I think it's a great idea."

Except that Hawk wasn't exactly a relatable personality.

"I do have to agree with Emily on one point. There is a war on." Katie jumped into the conversation. "Hawkins is a professional soldier and is already over there. But we'd have to send over Emily and at least one cameraman, ideally two, one for still shots and one for video. As untrained civilians, can we keep all of them safe? I've heard conditions can get pretty bad in some spots."

Emily's hopes rose. If anyone could get them out of this mess, it was Katie. Though when she considered the dangers in Afghanistan, she had to think that living in New York City was probably pretty good training.

"The USO sends people to the war zone all the time." Todd suddenly decided to join the conversation. He was obviously feeling bold since Emily, also an assistant, had spoken up earlier. "They send important people too. Celebrities. Comedians. And there are always bands and singers over there performing for the troops at their bases."

Emily frowned at him, silently willing him to shut up.

The last thing she had expected was to ever see Hawk again. After one short reply to her email, the bastard hadn't even bothered to contact her to say he was still alive.

Given that, she wasn't in any rush to fly to Afghanistan and have to work with him. He obviously didn't want to talk to her or he would have.

Besides avoiding further bruising to her already wounded ego, flying into the middle of the war hadn't been on her immediate agenda.

"Perfect. Great idea, Todd." Mr. Howard smiled at his underling, who glowed under the praise, probably while he envisioned getting his own big solo assignment and moving up in the company.

"Marci." Mr. Dean turned to his assistant who sat silently with her laptop open on the conference table clicking away as she took notes for him. "What can you find about the USO?"

Marci's fingers flew into action and—didn't it figure—she had the website up in no time.

"They're a not-for-profit, privately-owned organization. Ooo, this is good. They offer what they call a 'handshake tour'. Besides comedians and musical acts, they've had authors, sports figures and politicians on tour. Here's a picture of that bicyclist Lance Armstrong with the troops. It says they have a USO center set up at Bagram Air Base in Afghanistan."

"Where is our boy Hawk?" Mr. Dean asked Emily directly, shocking her out of her silence.

"Kabul," she reluctantly supplied, feeling her cheeks blush at the mention of *our* boy Hawk.

"Marci. How close is that to Bagram?" Mr. Dean asked.

"I think they're pretty close." Know-it-all Todd jumped in once again uninvited.

Emily sat silently as Marci's fingers clicked, knowing damn well after already obsessively studying the Afghan map that Bagram and Kabul were very close, on the map at least.

Before Marci could tell them that, Emily's hand shot up again. "But Hawk isn't a celebrity like Lance Armstrong. Why would the soldiers want to shake hands with just another soldier?"

Mr. Howard answered her, "We're not trying to make Hawk a celebrity among other soldiers, but we do want them to relate to him and feel good that he's representing them to the world. But more importantly, this tour is a photo op. It's for the people back home who need to feel good about where their young men and women and hard earned tax dollars are going. Photos and videos of him there, properly placed in the media here at home, will accomplish that."

"Bagram Air Base is an hour drive north of the capital city of Kabul, Mr. Dean." Marci looked absolutely gleeful at finding that out for her boss.

Damned efficient Marci.

This could not happen. They had agreed in the bar before any of the incredible sex they would never see each other again. He hadn't made contact since landing in Afghanistan so she had to assume he hadn't changed his mind.

Emily couldn't face seeing Hawk and having him blow her off. Not after he'd occupied her mind night and day for weeks. Besides that, he didn't even want his men to know about the print ads, and now her bosses wanted him to conduct a celebrity handshake tour.

He'd flip out over that and probably take it out on her. She had to stop this runaway train.

"Hawk isn't in the city. I believe he and his soldiers are in a primitive camp somewhere in the Kabul Province in the mountains along the Pakistan border." Emily realized too late that was an awful lot of information for her to have about a model she'd worked with only once.

Mr. Howard raised an eyebrow, his coffee mug poised halfway to his lips. "I take it you can get in touch with him somehow?"

Emily blanched. She'd emailed him once while he was still in Germany. After his one-word response, she'd had no intention of ever doing it again.

"Um, I don't know. I suppose so. I can try emailing him, but the satellite internet can be iffy there . . . I believe." Yeah, she didn't sound too much like she'd become a stalker and read everything she could get her hands on regarding the troops in that area. "But again, it will be up to his superiors to allow him to come to Bagram."

"The client is the US Army." Mr. Dean tapped his copy of the client folder on the conference table. "If they want their own campaign to succeed, I don't see that they'd have a problem working with us by loaning out one soldier for a few days."

"True," Mr. Howard agreed. "But it never hurts to cover all the bases when dealing with the military." He swiveled his chair to face Katie. "How about your contacts? Can you get this Hawk ordered to do a USO handshake tour?"

Katie smiled. "I'll call Hank Miller and see what he can do. That man is amazing when it comes to getting people to do things."

Mr. Howard donned a satisfied smile. He loved nothing more than pulling strings. "Excellent."

Smiling too, Mr. Dean nodded. "This might actually work out perfectly. If we can hook him up with a celebrity already on a scheduled tour, we can piggyback on their publicity and the troop support. There's our missing star power that we had with the Milano-SpecOps joint campaign. Marci, can you forward the USO information to Emily?"

"Already emailed. And they have contact information and phone numbers listed right here on the site."

Oh goody.

"Thanks, Marci." Emily tried to sound sincere.

Mr. Dean started shuffling papers into a pile and stashing them into various folders, which he shoved at Todd. "Emily? Can you handle coordinating the USO aspect?"

"Yes, sir. I'll get right on it."

"Great. Keep us informed." Mr. Dean clicking shut the latch on his briefcase sounded to Emily like the final nail in her coffin.

"This is an important client," Mr. Howard added, as if Emily didn't already know that paralyzing detail. "I want to be apprised every step of the way."

With that, Howard and Dean both rose and the meeting was over.

As the room emptied, Emily remained frozen in her seat.

This was going to happen. She would have to see him again, do her job and do it well and all while pretending that everything was perfectly okay.

For maybe the thousandth time since Germany, Emily revisited her and Hawk's final moments together.

"You going to be able to get back to the base okay?" she'd asked that morning, suitcase packed and zipped and ready to go to the airport.

"Yeah, I kept one of the cars we came in and made the rest of the guys cram into the other two." Hawk had run a hand up her arm to cup her face and then said, "You know, I've been thinking."

"Uh, oh. Are you sure that's safe? You thinking?" Emily had teased him to avoid tearing up at their parting.

He'd grinned at her then, and she remembered her heart skipping a beat. That was when she'd known saying goodbye and meaning it was not going to be so easy.

"I was thinking that it might be kind of cool if you did email me the pictures. I'd like to have them, you know, just for fun. Might be good for a laugh." Hawk's words had made her heart and her hopes surge.

She'd nodded. "Oh, sure. I can definitely do that. No problem."

Yeah, sure. No problem at all, except that she'd emailed him the pictures the moment her feet hit US soil and had gotten exactly one word back from him by email.

"Thanks." That was it.

And that was what she got for hoping, for planning, for thinking that an agreed upon one-night stand could be anything more.

"You gonna be okay with this? Em?"

Emily was yanked away from her memories with a jolt. She realized Katie had been talking to her.

"Hmm?"

"Going to Afghanistan, into a war zone. Are you okay with that?" Katie clarified when Emily gave her a blank stare.

"Oh yeah. I'm great. Actually, I've always wanted to see Afghanistan." Emily joked to cover her discomposure.

"You sure?" Concern was clear on Katie's face.

"Yeah. I'm sure." Compared to seeing Hawk again, the war was the least of Emily's worries.

"Are you going to email Hawk with the good news?"

The question was perfectly innocent. Katie knew nothing about Emily's night with Hawk. Katie had no clue how much she dreaded having to contact Hawk since she'd chosen to keep her little indiscretion in Germany to herself.

"Um, I think I'll get everything ironed out first with the USO and wait to get approval from the Army. No use getting Hawk involved if we might have to cancel."

With any luck they wouldn't get approval. Emily felt like a traitor to her company for wishing that, but it was true.

Katie nodded. "You're right. I'll be interested to see how the USO feels about our idea."

"Me too," Emily agreed. Her other question was exactly how angry was Hawk going to be about this? She was sure it wasn't going to be good.

CHAPTER SEVENTEEN

"Can I borrow your toothpaste later, Hawk?" Wally asked after a mouthful of food. "I'm out until my next care package gets here from Mama."

And until whenever the hell the next supply drop would arrive to deliver that care package . . .

Hawk sighed. "Yeah, sure."

Wally grinned. "Thanks. I've got an extra deodorant if you need it."

Hawk raised a brow. "Thanks."

If the temperature reached above freezing in the near future, Wally's antiperspirant might be a hot commodity, but at the moment the chance of sweating seemed pretty slim.

Personal items at their forward operating base in the Kabul Province were scarce, to put it mildly.

Hawk and his squad were far from anyone else, including the main part of their own unit. No base meant no store, which meant some basic necessities, things like toothpaste and, believe it or not, forks, were hard to come by.

Guys actually walked around with their forks in their pockets to make sure they didn't lose them or no one swiped them.

You pretty much had to come stocked with everything you would need, borrow from one of the other guys or do without until more arrived from home.

Hawk's camp was so remote that supplies were sling loaded beneath a chopper, flown in and then dropped. Unfortunately, you never knew when the supply drop would arrive. Or exactly where it would end up crashing to the ground.

It seemed the only convenience they did have on a regular basis was internet access. Go figure. A hell of a lot of good email did Hawk since he'd vowed to himself he wouldn't maintain contact with Emily while he was downrange.

Basically, it seemed the only things to do there were fight, write—for those who had someone to write to—clean weapons or reload mags. Fun stuff.

Oh, and think. There was far too much time to think. More often than not, Hawk's thoughts turned to Emily and their one night together. Then his mind went to that day right after they'd been together when she'd emailed him in Germany with his photos.

She'd kept the email all casual and light, on the surface anyway. Reading between the lines, Hawk could tell she wanted more. He could have a girlfriend if he wanted one. He knew he could have Emily if he wanted her.

Wanting wasn't the problem. This was not the time or place to get himself tied to a new girl back in the States.

Every moment of every day had to be spent making sure he brought his men home alive. After he'd accomplished that, God willing, he'd worry about the other parts of his life.

Hawk yanked his mind away from thoughts of Emily.

He stood and sent a meaningful look at Wally. "I'm gonna go get on the computer and email my sister for some toothpaste. Looks like I'll be needing some more soon."

"Ask her to send some pictures of herself too." Wally grinned and waggled his eyebrows.

The man knew exactly how to push Hawk's buttons. Hawk ignored him. Hopefully, like an ill-behaved child, Wally would give up if he didn't get a reaction.

With a sigh, Hawk threw away his empty MRE package—

meals ready to eat being their main sustenance nowadays—and left his men to finish their respective meals.

He made his way to the tent where the shared computer was located. Since the rest of the guys were still eating, he was alone as he logged into his email account. He owed his sister an email anyway or there would be hell to pay.

It was just easier to shoot her a quick hello than listen to her bitch for the rest of his life.

As expected, an email from her sat in his inbox. *Would be nice to know my brother is alive and well. Write me! Susan*

Also, as per usual, were a good dozen jokes, pictures or funny videos sent to him by the guys back at the rear. Hawk deleted most of those without reading them.

Buried below all the others, one message had his hand pausing on the mouse as his pulse sped.

After all this time, there was an email from Emily. Hawk clicked it open. He found himself leaning closer to the screen to read it.

Hawk. You'll be getting orders for another assignment. I swear I did my best to get you out of it. Sorry. Emily.

What the hell? Orders for another modeling assignment? Out here?

Hawk laughed. If they could get those orders to him through the snowdrifts, he'd gladly follow them. Emily probably wanted a picture of him in his white snow camo *outfit*.

She'd have him standing outside in a blizzard for some new ad, as if that would make the young boys and girls back home jump right up and run to the local recruiting office to enlist.

Since it was doubtful they were sending Rasta-photographer here to him, Hawk figured whatever pictures she needed he could have Pettit take.

Hawk would have Pettit snap a few shots with that super expensive digital camera the man was so proud of. Then he'd email the pictures to Emily and be done with it. That should cover it.

Confident that was all this new assignment would entail, Hawk sent a quick reply to his sister, remembering to ask her to send him toothpaste, and a package of plastic forks if she had the time to pick them up. Then he emptied all the remaining emails out of his inbox and logged off.

Back in his tent, Hawk broke down his weapon and took out the gun oil and supplies he'd need. He settled in for the meticulous job of cleaning the familiar item.

The act was almost like meditation for him. As his hands completed the task they knew so well, he let his mind wander. As usual, Emily was the main attraction. Hawk laughed as he imagined Emily's horror at having to ask him for more pictures when she knew how unhappy he'd been about the first set.

His mind would have no doubt turned to some of his more intimate memories of Emily except for the sound— far in the distance—that caught his attention.

The familiar *whoop whoop whoop* of blades cutting air had him on immediate alert. Hawk snapped his gaze to locate his backup weapon as he slammed the pieces of the gun in his hand back together.

Outside someone, it sounded like Wally, shouted, "Woo hoo! Mail call."

Not an attack. Hawk relaxed.

Slamming the last piece of his cleaned and oiled weapon into place, Hawk flung it over his shoulder and went out to see what goodies had been delivered.

Hopefully Wally's care package with his toothpaste and maybe even Hawk's mysterious new orders would be among the packages and letters.

He chuckled again and thought of Emily trying to get him out of the new assignment. If she was working that hard to keep him happy, perhaps she wasn't too angry with him and his lack of communications after all.

CHAPTER EIGHTEEN

In her peripheral vision, Emily noticed Jai glancing at her once again, just like he'd been doing for most of the flight. "What?"

Jai shrugged. "Nothing. You just seem nervous."

"I'm not nervous." That said, Emily noticed she'd been drumming her fingers on the armrest between their two seats and immediately folded both hands in her lap over her seat belt.

"It's perfectly understandable, Em. You're flying to Afghanistan. The war may have begun centered in Iraq, but there's a major threat in Afghanistan. It's no picnic. I remember my first time here. It can be scary, and even more so for you, being a woman."

She rolled her eyes. "We're going to be on a US base full of armed men. I'm not worried I'll be taken hostage by the local gun-toting bad guys. Honestly."

It was only one guy who had her on edge. Hawk.

"Hmm." Jai's doubt was clearly evident in that one sound.

She turned in her narrow commercial-airplane seat to face Jai. "Yes? Do you have more to say?"

Even in business class, the seats weren't exactly comfortable for the length of time they'd been in them. But right now, Jai was even more annoying than Emily's seat and the stiffness in her legs.

"I was just remembering the flight home from Germany. You were a little freaky then too, exhausted and hyper at the same time."

Memories of why that was true hit her hard. She threw up her defenses to distract Jai. "I'm not afraid of flying if that's what you're saying."

"No, I know it's not fear of flying. I've flown with you before and you were fine. But there's something . . ." Realization dawned on his face. "It's him. You're nervous about seeing him again."

She felt her face blanch. "I don't know who you're talking about."

Emily looked anywhere except at Jai. She was such a bad liar that people always saw right through her, and she didn't need Jai knowing the truth. Not now on the way to see Hawk again when she was already beyond stressed.

"Oh my God. You had sex with Hawk that last night in Germany. The night we went to the bar and he was there."

Emily nearly choked. Was it written that clearly across her face? "What? No, of course not."

"I can't believe I didn't realize it before." Jai continued, studying her face as she felt it grow hot.

"Jai, I don't know what you're talking about."

"Em, come on." He let out a long, slow hiss of breath. "The sexual tension between you and Hawk during those photo shoots and then at the bar was so thick I could have cut it with a knife. I just never imagined you'd actually . . . Wow. You and Hawk."

Heart pounding, Emily started to deny it some more but instead sank low in her seat, defeated. "You must think so badly of me."

Frowning, Jai let out a short laugh. "Why?"

"I barely knew him."

"Oh jeez, Em. Do you know what I see on the road with all those models and crew? One-night stands are tame compared to the orgies, drugs, alcohol—you name it and I've seen it. I'm glad you finally let yourself relax for a night. And falling for a really nice guy is nothing to be ashamed of."

"You think Hawk is nice?" That out of all the rest surprised her the most.

"Yeah. I mean, in a tough-guy trained-killer kind of way. He's a good guy."

"How do you know?" she asked.

"I spent time with his squad at the Ratskeller after both you and Hawk mysteriously got tired about the same time and went to bed." Jai obviously realized now that excuse had been a big old fib.

She rubbed her hands over her face. "I told him to wait awhile so it wouldn't look suspicious."

"Oh, he did. Hawk waited a good three minutes." Jai grinned. "Anyway, I can tell you his men love him. You want some guy advice, Em?"

Emily guessed it couldn't hurt. "Sure."

"If you want to know if a man is worth your time, you look at how he treats others and how they treat him, particularly his subordinates. Hawk's a decent man. A bit serious at times, but still, you could have done far worse than him to jump in bed with."

Emily sighed. As much as she would love to tell Jai how wrong he was about Hawk, she couldn't bring herself to admit he hadn't even bothered to email her after she wrote him about this newest assignment.

Hawk may well be a good guy to his soldiers. She'd freely admit that, but so what if he was a man's man? In the female department, and at communicating, the man was severely lacking.

In fact, he just plain sucked. Nice guys returned emails. Case closed.

"Can we change the subject now?" She shot Jai a sideways glance.

He smirked but nodded. "Sure. Hmm. Let's see. Subject change. Oh, I know. So what do you think of Miss USO up there?" Jai suggested the new topic of conversation in a low whisper.

"I think, judging from the looks of her outfit, the soldiers at Bagram are going to be very happy to see her." Emily wasn't so considerate and used her natural voice level, figuring Little Miss USO and her entourage probably couldn't hear. Not from their seats all the way up there in first class where she was probably drinking bottles of complimentary champagne.

Honestly, a sequined top for a plane ride to Afghanistan?

"She's an entertainer, Emily. They all act a bit over the top. It's just part of the image. You know, packaging for the public."

Emily raised a brow, thinking that the *packaging* had a little help from a bottle of red hair dye and some silicone implants, not to mention a press person, makeup and hair person and a bruiser of a bodyguard.

"So you're saying the fact she flirted with you is all part of the act?"

Jai grinned. "Nope, that was all part of my charm."

"And what about her flirting with the pilot, the man who took our boarding passes and even the male flight attendant? Hmm?" Emily challenged.

"She did? I'm crushed." Jai feigned shock, and then laughed at Emily's scowl. "All right, I'll admit it. She is a bit flirty."

And Hawk was scheduled to be at her side every step of his time in Bagram. Just great.

Emily imagined all the flirting, or worse, Little Miss USO would do with Hawk and how he'd eat it right up. She let out a low groan.

"Oh, lighten up, Em. This being part of a USO tour will be fun. You'll see."

Emily scowled. "Oh yeah, real fun. I can't wait."

CHAPTER NINETEEN

Emily's love for Kerri London, chart-topping country singer and star of this USO thing, did not grow during the twenty-two-hour journey.

In fact, by the time their plane landed in Afghanistan and Emily waited in the aisle for what seemed like forever for Little Miss USO's entourage to get all of her many carry-ons out of the overhead compartments, she was seething.

"Some people are so inconsiderate. Why the hell didn't she check all that stuff with the regular luggage instead of carrying it on?"

Jai glanced down at Emily's laptop case and additional carry-on, along with her neck pillow, wool wrap and water bottle and raised an eyebrow.

"I needed this stuff to work on the flight," she defended against his unspoken condemnation.

So what if she'd been so nervous about seeing Hawk again she hadn't done a damn bit of work? She'd intended to and that's all that counted.

Jai laughed. "Okay, if you say so. Come on. It looks like we're moving. I've had enough of riding around in this tin can."

"Hmm. A bit of claustrophobia?" Emily jumped on the opportunity to pay Jai back for his teasing of her.

He shot her a look. "I admit nothing. And before you start

picking on me, let's see how you fare on your first helicopter ride, shall we?"

Jai headed down the aisle. Emily followed a bit less enthusiastically. She'd thought the incredibly long and many-legged trip to the airport in Kabul had been bad. But she had a feeling the relatively short helicopter ride to the military airport at Bagram Air Base would probably be far worse.

It turned out she was right in that prediction. White knuckled the entire time, Emily managed to not lose her lunch or pass out during her first helicopter ride, but she was shaking like a leaf by the time they got off. Jai on the other hand, didn't seem to mind it at all.

"So you don't like being on a huge commercial jet, but you didn't mind this flying eggbeater? Why is that?" She frowned as she stumbled after him on wobbly legs across the airfield.

Jai shrugged. "We all have our little quirks. And that huge commercial jet, as you put it, doesn't feel so huge when you're as tall as I am. My legs are still cramped. Next trip, we're going to have to get the big guys to spring for first class."

She let out a laugh. "Yeah, good luck. Maybe for talent but not for us."

Speaking of first class . . . Emily glanced back at Little Miss USO. She was doing just fine as both her bodyguard and some military guy helped her out of the helicopter.

That figured. Emily probably could have fallen out on her face and they would barely have noticed. She glanced down at her own comparatively diminutive chest, figuring that must be the differentiating factor.

With a sigh of resignation, Emily looked ahead and noticed Jai had gotten pretty far in front of her. He strode toward a smiling, sandy-haired man. She rushed to catch up.

"Hey! Mel. Good to see you." Jai greeted the man like they were old friends.

"Jai." The stranger responded with a handshake and a slap on Jai's back.

Emily frowned at him. "You two know each other?"

"Sure do. I'm sorry, Em. Let me introduce you. Emily Price, marketing maven from Madison Avenue's famed Howard & Dean Agency. Mel Townsend, Australia's best embedded-combat video man."

Emily extended her hand. "Australia? Wow. When I asked Jai if he knew any cameramen for this assignment, I didn't realize his little black book extended to another hemisphere."

Smiling, Mel shook her hand. "Jai and me, we've known each other for years. Since— "

"Kandahar, two thousand and four," Jai finished for him. When he noticed Emily's surprised look, he shrugged. "I told you I've been to Afghanistan before."

She drew her brows closer together as she considered she really didn't know much about Jai at all. She'd always just assumed he'd stuck with magazine-fashion layouts with the occasional ad shoots thrown in. She needed to pay more attention.

"That's right. That was a hell of an assignment." Mel grinned.

"Mel's been embedded in Afghanistan with the 82nd Airborne along with an Aussie reporter for the past six months. When I found out he was here on his own because the reporter he was assigned to shipped home, I contacted him."

"And I said bloody hell, yes, I would gladly work with this old bastard again, especially for this assignment. She's sweet. Easy peasy. Aye, Jai?"

"Compared to some of our other assignments, oh yeah," Jai agreed with a snigger but didn't elaborate.

Emily watched the interaction with interest. Definitely some history there.

"I figure any assignment where the Humvee I'm riding in doesn't get blown up is apples." Mel laughed as he addressed Emily again.

Her eyes opened wide. "Is that very often? You getting blown up, I mean?"

The ruggedly handsome Australian grinned wider. Laugh

lines creased the corners of his whisky-colored eyes. "More often than I'd like, but no worries, Emmie. This assignment, she'll be right. We'll be safe."

"All righty. Good to hear." Emily nodded, wondering how her name had suddenly become Emmie.

"Any word on Hawkins's ETA?" Jai asked Emily.

She shrugged. "We don't have any events scheduled for the handshake tour until tomorrow. He's supposed to arrive sometime today, but you know the military—when they do give you a timeframe, they change it ten times. I guess we have to trust the Army will get him here."

"He'll be here today." Mel nodded. "His helo should be arriving any tic of the clock now. I talked to some of the blokes in the control tower."

Emily raised a brow that Mel could get an answer so easily when all she'd gotten from the military for the past week was the runaround.

"Holy moly. Who's the stunner? She the star of this show?" Mel elbowed Jai in the side and stared in Miss USO's direction.

"Yup. That's Kerri London herself." With a sideways glance at Emily, Jai added, "She and Emily are going to be good friends by the end of this tour. I can tell already."

Emily shot him a nasty look before watching the object of all the male attention make her way across the airfield in skintight red leather pants, four-inch heels and a rhinestone studded denim jacket over her tube top. Her long red mane blew in the wind.

Mel continued to look in Kerri London's direction. "She does look like she's keen to get a bit. But don't you worry, Emmie. She's got nothing on you. Besides, there are more than enough diggers around here for both of you, plus some."

Emily frowned. "What's a digger?"

"Military men," Jai supplied.

She was beginning to feel as though she needed a translator, or at least an Australian/American dictionary, to speak to Mel. Even so, she got the drift of his last statement and scowled.

"I am here to work, not find men." *Or diggers.*

That statement was truthful. She wasn't looking for men, only for one particular man, and she was dreading seeing him.

Emily watched the wide sway of Kerri London's shapely hips and the energetic bounce of her more-than-generous chest and sighed.

This woman had all the assets Hawk would appreciate. Watching Hawk hook up with Miss Sex on Heels after she'd been with him might be more than Emily could take.

Mel's arm around her shoulders drew her attention back to him. "Come on, love. Your friend over there has her own transportation. I'll be driving you and Jai. Let's get your things and you loaded into my jeep. You keen for some tucker or a cuppa?"

Emily wasn't sure if she was keen for some tucker or not and was afraid to answer lest she commit herself to an orgy with some diggers or something.

With a silent plea, she raised a brow and glanced at Jai.

Laughing out loud, Jai answered her unspoken question, "He means food and a cup of something hot to drink, Em. You'll get used to him, don't worry."

Somehow, Emily doubted that. But his offer reminded her how chilled she'd become from the helicopter ride and from standing in the wind on the airfield.

"Sure, Mel. Some food and hot coffee would be great." And getting away from Ms. Kerri *Hot Pants* London even better.

"Good, and then I can show you to your lush accommodations for the duration of your stay." With a wink at Jai, Mel asked, "So, Emmie, have you ever slept in a tent before?"

Emily groaned. This was going to be one heck of a trip.

CHAPTER TWENTY

"So, Grandpa. How are they still letting you fly? I'd thought you'd be back in the nursing home by now." Wally grinned as he joked with the helicopter pilot.

"Listen here, boy. I was flying when you weren't even a gleam in your mama's eye and I'm still here. What does that tell you?"

"That the Army is desperate and has to hit up the senior citizen centers back in the States to recruit?" Wally shot back with a smirk.

"Ha, ha. Real funny there, kid."

The pilot was the same one who'd brought Hawk and the squad to their secluded camp weeks before. So far, the elder man gave as good as he got from Wally, which never failed to amuse Hawk.

The man had to be pushing sixty. He'd flown CH-46s for the Marines during the final years of the Vietnam War. The reality was that the wrinkled, gray-haired reservist was nearing the upper age limit to be allowed to fly and would soon have to retire, but the old coot was determined not to quit before they forced him out. For that, Hawk had to admire him.

In any case, it was nice to see any familiar face again out here, even one he'd only met once.

Hawk smiled at the pilot. "Good to see you again, Lou."

"You too, Hawk. Didn't think I'd be picking you up again so soon. What's up? You and your two boys here giving up already and heading for home?"

Hawk snorted out a laugh. "Not exactly." He almost wished that were the case rather than the real reason he was here.

"I'll tell you what, it's way better than that, Grandpa. Well, maybe not better than going home but still really great. Wait until you hear the news." His excitement evident, Wally practically bounced in his combat boots.

"Wally. " Hawk growled in warning.

"What? I can tell him about my promotion, can't I?" Wally looked innocently at Hawk. A bit too innocently.

"Yes, you can tell him about your promotion." Hawk grit his teeth, willing Wally not to spill the rest of the news. The news about the recent orders that had Hawk far from happy.

It seemed Hawk's captain and his good old friend Commander Hank Miller had been busy in the weeks Hawk and his squad had been downrange. Between the two of them, and thanks to some marketing geniuses, Hawk was now part of a frigging USO handshake tour with a country singer he'd never heard of.

But that wasn't even the worst part. Thanks to a strange twist of fate, Wally's advancement had come through from the promotions board. Someone decided it would be good press to incorporate the promotion ceremony into the tour.

Of all people, now big-mouthed Wally was in on Hawk's modeling secret, and Hawk had a horrible feeling that would cost him. He'd probably have to barter his sister for Wally's secrecy.

Traveling conditions in the area were volatile enough that Hawk was instructed to take both Wally and another soldier with him. Pettit had been the no-brainer decision since he was already privy to Hawk's secret hell.

Hawk had left Specialist Black from Alpha team in charge of his remaining men.

So here they were, the three amigos, heading for a frigging USO tour.

Hawk wrestled himself out of his own misery and listened as Wally told Lou his news.

"I finally made it, Grandpa. No more Specialist Trent Wallace. When you fly us back, you'll have to call me sergeant."

"You'll be lucky if I don't call you the one who accidentally fell out of the chopper." The old pilot was so amused at his own joke he laughed until he coughed so hard he had to snub out his cigarette.

As the pilot lit up another one, Hawk smiled at the single bright spot to this trip—the fact the old coot took no shit from Wally. Though Hawk feared that unless he decided to pull rank on Wally, he would certainly have to take some shit from him about this modeling gig.

Hawk considered that in under an hour he'd be with Emily again. Okay, maybe that made two bright spots in this trip.

He'd get to see Emily after what seemed like a very long separation and find out if this near-physical ache he felt whenever he was alone and thinking about her was strictly a combination of sexual deprivation and the loneliness of being deployed, or the real thing.

He was really hoping it was the former. This was neither the time nor the place for the real thing.

CHAPTER TWENTY-ONE

Taking a long sip, Emily was enjoying a nice steaming hot *cuppa* in the dining hall with Jai and her new Aussie pal when she felt *his* presence.

Jai's wave in the direction of the door at her back confirmed her intuition. She knew without turning around Hawk had arrived. Her heart kicked into double time. She didn't think that was caused by the caffeine.

A trio of men strode as one into her line of sight to stand next to the long table.

"Sergeant. Glad to see you made it," Jai greeted.

Emily knew the moment had come. She would have to speak to Hawk too, yet she still didn't know how she should act.

Angry? Which she was. Indifferent? Even though her heart pounded hard enough to vibrate her chest. Cool and friendly like nothing had happened between them? That would require an award-winning performance on her part.

She had no clue what to do or say. Worse, she'd begun to wonder if her voice would give her away no matter what words she chose.

Luckily for Emily, Jai made the introductions and gave her a small reprieve.

"Mel, this is our man for the shoot, Staff Sergeant

Hawkins. Sergeant Hawkins, meet Mel Townsend, our video man for the next few days."

Mel rose and shook Hawk's hand. "G'day, mate."

"Sergeant Ryan Pettit and Specialist Trent Wallace." Hawk hooked a thumb at each of the two men on either side of him as he introduced them.

"Call me Wally. And after tomorrow, it'll be Sergeant instead of Specialist," one of Hawk's entourage added.

Feeling ridiculous that she had yet to speak, Emily jumped in. "I saw your captain had added the promotion ceremony to the schedule of events. Congratulations, Wally."

That earned her a wide grin from the man. Paranoid, Emily had the bad feeling Wally recognized her from the Ratskeller and was imagining how exactly his sergeant and she had spent that night in Germany.

Wally took a step closer and, smiling, extended one beefy hand in her direction. "Well, hello there."

"Wally." The warning in Hawk's voice was evident.

"Just being friendly." Wally grinned as he took Emily's offered hand in both of his and shook it. "Polite and friendly like my mama taught me."

"Your mama didn't teach you what you're thinking." Hawk took a step closer to them both.

Wally dropped her hand in response and took a step back, conceding to Hawk. That was both interesting and maddening at the same time. Hawk hadn't made any attempt to contact her since that one-word email right after Germany, but in true caveman fashion, he had sent a definite signal to Wally to back off.

Hawk might as well have peed on her leg like a damn male dog and marked her as his territory.

Apparently he didn't want her but no one else could have her either. Lovely. But actually, knowing Hawk, not that surprising.

Emily couldn't avoid it any longer. She finally looked directly into Hawk's gaze, finding it focused singly on her.

He smiled. "Hey there, Goldilocks."

The deep timbre of his voice and his small crooked smile melted her frozen heart, while at the same time reignited her anger. Particularly when Emily noted she was back to being Goldilocks again, reaffirming that any closeness they'd gained that one night in Germany had expired.

"Hi, Hawk. Glad to see you're still alive." Emily answered as flippantly as she could.

He smirked at that. "It takes a lot to kill me, doll."

Of that, she was certain, at least at those times when she was royally pissed off at him, like now. During other times, when she forgot to be angry, believing Hawk would be hard to kill didn't do much to ease all those ridiculously pointless nights of worrying she'd had over this man.

Meanwhile, Hawk probably hadn't given her a second thought since they'd said goodbye in her hotel room.

Feeling mean, she smiled sweetly back. "Good, because I'd hate to have to start the ad campaign from scratch with a new model. So much work . . ." She shook her head.

Hawk laughed and Emily couldn't help but notice the adorable way crinkles appeared around his eyes. She batted away the flutter in her belly simply looking at him caused.

Wally raised his hand to get her attention. "I'm available to model if you need me, Ms. Price."

"No, you're not." Hawk's eyes never left her face.

Wally nodded and mouthed behind Hawk's back, "Call me."

"Nice to see you both again, Miss Price, Mr. Devereaux." Pettit, ever polite, stepped forward and shook her hand and Jai's. Then he turned to Mel. "Very nice to meet you, Mr. Townsend."

"Pleasure's mine, Sergeant." Mel pumped Pettit's hand.

The male bonding and testosterone level surrounding her was starting to stifle her. She needed something to do. She was starting to feel uncomfortable under Hawk's constant gaze. "Well, great. Now that everyone's been introduced perhaps we should review the schedule."

"No need. I've got the schedule." Hawk held up a folded

piece of paper he'd had hidden somewhere in his uniform. "It's simple enough. I'll be where I'm supposed to, when I'm supposed to be there. Don't worry."

"I wasn't worried," she bit out.

"No?" Hawk raised a brow skeptically.

She hated he knew her so well, even if they'd only worked together for two days. Not reviewing the schedule with all the parties involved would up her stress level considerably and Hawk darn well knew it.

Emily was considering how to suggest again they all go over the schedule together while not sounding obsessive compulsive, thereby proving Hawk right, when she noticed she was the subject of Jai's smirk and Mel's interested stare.

If she weren't careful, not only Jai, but also Mel would know about her little indiscretion with Hawk.

"Um, Jai. Don't you think we need to review the schedule with Mel?" Emily suggested.

Jai raised a brow in her direction. He had worked with her enough to know her obsessive organizational issues. Emily felt fairly certain that it was becoming obvious to Mel also. Was she that transparent to the entire male race?

"Why yes, Emily. I think it's an excellent idea to go over things with Mel. Sergeant, would you and your men like to join us while we brief our new cameraman?" Jai was humoring her. She didn't care. She had too many other issues to deal with.

Hawk nodded. "Sure. Just let us grab some chow."

"We'll be right back." Wally spoke specifically to Emily with a wink and a grin.

She couldn't help but laugh, especially when she saw Hawk set his jaw.

"Okay, we'll wait for you," she said, amused.

Hawk, Wally and Pettit left, and when the overwhelming presence that was Hawk moved farther away, Emily could finally breathe freely for the first time in minutes.

"So, you and the staff sergeant, huh?" Mel grinned.

"Jai." Emily squealed the accusation, spinning to frown at

him.

"What? I didn't tell him. My hand to God, Emily, I swear." Jai held up one hand in defense.

"Don't blame him, Emmie. Jai didn't tell me. You did. You should never play poker. You don't have the face for it."

Emily sighed. No use hiding it now.

Mel continued, "In any case, whatever happened or didn't happen doesn't matter. There sure is a good bit of tension between you two now."

That was a huge understatement.

"Yeah, there is. I just don't get how he can act like I'm his territory. Did you see him with Wally? What's up with that?"

Jai shrugged. "He's just being a man."

Mel nodded. "And if you use it to your advantage, Emmie, he'll play directly into your hands."

She was about to protest that maybe she didn't want him in her hands when further conversation was interrupted because Hawk and his men returned, trays of food in hand.

Changing the subject, Emily grabbed her bag from the floor. "Okay, let's get started."

"Super. So what have you got for me, love?" Scooting his chair closer, Mel hooked an arm around the back of Emily's chair. He ran his fingers lightly up and down her arm.

It took Emily a moment to recover from the shock of that. But after one look at his wicked grin and his wink, she realized Mel was trying to make Hawk jealous. For her benefit or just to piss off Hawk she wasn't sure.

As petty as Emily felt right now, she kind of liked that idea. It would serve him right. Maybe if he had bothered to email her, things could have been different.

Emily glanced in Hawk's direction. His gaze remained focused on Mel's fingers still touching her.

Pettit and Wally attacked their food like starving men while Hawk had yet to touch his. She was certain jealousy was practically killing the man.

As his face grew stonier by the second, Emily really began to fear for Mel's wellbeing. She shot a glance at Jai who looked amused by the whole turn of events. No help there.

Deciding there was nothing she could do about it now without making a scene, she ignored Mel and his wandering fingers, refused to look at Hawk and his possessive anger and took out her papers to review the schedule.

When all else failed, resort to work mode. That was Emily's usual *modus operandi* in times of personal crisis, and she saw no need to change it now.

She focused solely on the paper in front of her. "Okay. First thing after breakfast with the troops tomorrow morning is Wally's promotion ceremony . . ."

CHAPTER TWENTY-TWO

Hawk was sure he was going to need dental work by the time he left Bagram. Since he'd arrived, he'd kept his jaw clenched in an attempt to not tell that damn Aussie to get his fucking hands off Emily.

The cameraman had been all over her at dinner, then even worse the next morning. The bastard had the nerve to kiss her cheek at breakfast, leaving Hawk to wonder precisely where he'd spent the night.

Exactly how long had Emily and Crocodile Dundee been here in Bagram together? Hawk didn't know, but he sure as hell wanted to find out.

In spite of their history together, or maybe because of it, Hawk would never take Emily as the kind who would sleep around with a guy she'd just met. He knew he'd been the exception in Germany, not the rule. But damn, with this guy anything was possible.

She might see the Aussie as different. Smooth-talking foreigners were sexy to women. Not that Hawk could judge that kind of shit in other men, but chicks always dug guys with foreign accents.

The possibility of Emily being with this Mel Townsend character was all Hawk could think about. And now he had to participate in Wally's promotion ceremony in front of a hundred and fifty, maybe two hundred soldiers and act like nothing was wrong.

Though they weren't there for him or Wally. They were there to get a look at this supposedly famous singer.

Wally leaned closer. "I can't believe Kerri London is going to help promote me."

"You've heard of her?" Hawk looked at Wally, surprised.

"Hell, yeah. You haven't? Oh, come on, Hawk. You've heard her songs. I'm sure of it. 'Red Lipstick and a New Pair of Shoes'?"

Hawk raised a brow. "Must have missed that one."

"'Only Your Dog Loves You Now'?" Wally threw out another song title, or at least what Hawk assumed was a song.

He laughed. "Nope. Sorry. But that sounds like a good one."

Wally let out a frustrated sigh. "What do you listen to?"

"Your bitching, mostly." Hawk grinned until the officer who'd be promoting Wally climbed the stairs. He and Wally stood at attention.

The red-lipstick-wearing star herself preceded the officer onto the makeshift wooden stage. At least they'd put her in a flak jacket. Perhaps with her covered up a bit, Wally would be able to avoid drooling on her during the ceremony.

"Attention to orders!" The sound reverberated through the crowd.

In unison, the gathering of soldiers on the ground in front of the stage snapped firmly to attention.

A few hundred men in formation, all in their ACUs looking sharp and professional—that sight should make Emily happy for her shot.

He located her blonde head and cute figure in the crowd. Then he found that bastard Aussie cameraman next to her and scowled.

Hawk forced down the anger and made himself pay attention as the ceremony began and the officer read the promotion warrant.

"The Secretary of the Army has reposed special trust and

confidence in the patriotism, valor, fidelity and professional excellence of Trent Shirley Wallace . . ."

Shirley? Hawk somehow controlled his expression at that, but Wally was never going to hear the end of it that his middle name was Shirley.

He had to control his grin that he now had insurance and renewed faith in Wally's discretion regarding the modeling assignment because Hawk had something equally embarrassing on him.

The reading of the warrant continued.

"In view of these qualities and his demonstrated leadership potential and dedicated service to the US Army, he is therefore promoted from specialist to sergeant."

For the final piece of the promotion, the officer who'd read the warrant whispered instructions to the singer, who, to Wally's great pleasure Hawk was certain, personally attached his new stripes onto his uniform.

"Congratulations, Sergeant Wallace," she cooed to the accompaniment of a few camera flashes and the collective cheer of the assembly.

The promotion part of this gig was over, but unfortunately Hawk's job was far from done. Next came the picture-taking part of the program.

Every one of those many soldiers standing out in the cold was here not for Wally or Hawk, but rather to get his picture taken with Kerri London. Hawk was supposed to stand next to her for each and every shot whether they wanted him there or not.

"Hey there, sugar. Sorry we didn't get to meet earlier. I'm Kerri."

Hawk glanced down at her now as she addressed him directly. He shook her extended hand. "I'm Staff Sergeant David Hawkins."

Kerri raised one thin eyebrow and smiled seductively. "That's a mouthful, darlin', although I'm sure you are just that. What should I call you?"

Hawk raised a brow of his own. "You can call me Hawk."

"Hawk. I like that." She'd said his name as if she were trying out the feel of it on her tongue before turning toward Wally. "Now, Sergeant Trent Shirley Wallace. Since you're the man of the hour, you get your picture made first."

She flashed a smile at Wally, who visibly melted beneath her gaze.

"Shirley's a family name, ma'am. My mama's maiden name. We take family seriously where I'm from." Wally pressed so close to Kerri for the pose they looked glued at the hip.

"A fine man such as yourself, I'm sure you do take family serious, sugar. Now smile pretty for the camera."

Rasta-photographer motioned for Hawk to step closer to her. He did, though leaving a good six inches between his leg and hers. The Army photographer the USO had brought in for this tour stood next to Rasta and snapped away. Hawk's damn face was going to be everywhere. He sighed at the thought.

The snap of the camera heralded one picture down, two hundred or so more to go.

Actually, the entire process took less time than Hawk anticipated. He thought they'd be there until dinner considering Kerri took the time to personally flirt with each and every one of the men who climbed the stairs to stand next to her for a picture.

By the end, if Hawk never heard the words *sugar* or *smile* again, it would be too soon.

When the long line of soldiers finally disappeared and Kerri and Hawk were left alone on stage with no one but the photographer, the woman still amazingly had the capacity to smile at him.

"Well, thank you, Hawk. It was nice to have company for this one. I'm usually alone."

He somehow doubted Ms. Kerri London was ever alone unless she wanted to be.

Hawk had to laugh. "We both know not one of those soldiers was here to have their picture taken with me. They're probably cutting me out of the prints with their knives as we speak."

She laughed and smacked his chest playfully. "You're a funny one. But I can tell you I wouldn't be throwing your photo away. I bet just your picture could keep a girl warm at night."

Shaking his head at her, his own embarrassment surprised him.

Hawk broke eye contact with Kerri and noticed Emily next to the stage. She was telling Rasta-photographer and Crocodile Dundee something, but judging from the look on her face as she noticed Kerri touching him, she was pissed.

That was interesting . . .

Not one to look a gift horse in the mouth, Hawk played right into her jealousy. "Maybe we should have the photographer snap a shot of just the two of us. One copy for you and one for me. What do you say, Ms. London?"

"I'd love that, sugar. But only if you call me Kerri."

"You got it, Kerri." From the corner of his eye he watched Emily's face redden.

He draped one arm around the star, and for the first one of all those many, many pictures, Hawk actually smiled. He wasn't usually one to play games, but sometimes, such as now, it might be necessary.

Emily may be pissed, she might even be sleeping with the Aussie, but he knew one thing for certain, he wouldn't squander the second chance he'd been handed to be with her. They'd been thrown together again for this USO thing by fate or luck or frigging Dalton for all he knew. But whoever or whatever had put them together, Hawk wouldn't waste the opportunity.

Disengaging from Kerri, Hawk turned toward a seething Emily. "Okay, boss. What's next on the agenda?"

He knew exactly what was on the schedule. It was a tour of the base facilities, but he wanted Emily to have to talk to him.

Emily shot him a withering look that might wilt a less

determined man. "I don't know. Ask Jai."

Hawk hid his smile. She knew. She had that schedule memorized, just like he did. She was just too mad to answer him.

Yup, this jealousy thing just might work to his advantage.

Loud enough so Emily would hear, Hawk said, "Come on, Kerri. Off to our next stop." He extended his hand to help the singer down the steps just as Emily turned in a huff and stalked away.

Hawk watched her go and grinned. He always did enjoy a challenge. If nothing else, winning a fuming Emily back from the Aussie would be that.

"Bring it on."

"You say something, Hawk?" Kerri was nearer to him than he'd realized.

"Hmm? Oh, sorry. I'm just talking to myself. Bad habit I picked up from being deployed so much. You ready for our tour?"

"Ready and willing, sugar." She winked and extended her arm for him to take.

Strolling arm in arm with her, like the gentleman he sometimes pretended to be, Hawk shook his head at himself.

In the not-so-distant past, this woman would have been right up his alley. A hot and willing redhead, a pre-set and definite date of departure, deployment as the ideal excuse to not call her again . . . It was the perfect set-up for a short lived hot and heavy fling and Hawk wasn't at all interested.

What caused this sudden change of heart—or at least taste in women? He glanced up and saw Emily's irate, quick stride ahead of them and Hawk figured he already knew the answer to that.

CHAPTER TWENTY-THREE

Emily stared down at her copy of the schedule on the desk. One more day for a few more staged photo ops and then back to New York.

She wasn't sure if she was happy to get away from having to watch Hawk with that harpy or not. After this tour was over, she'd likely never see the man again. She was angry but that thought still hurt.

"I told you before. You keep frowning like that and you're gonna get wrinkles." His deep, achingly familiar voice filled the room.

She cursed herself for leaving the door to the office open so he could sneak up on her. Hawk stepped inside and swung that door closed, then strode directly to stand behind her chair.

Leaning down he planted a hand on the desk on each side of her and she was caged by his massive forearms.

"I thought we'd never be alone." Hawk spoke so close to Emily's ear, she could feel the warm heat of his breath on her skin.

His close proximity sent a shiver straight down her spine, which only made her frown deeper.

They were alone in the USO office she'd been allowed to use, and this late at night there wasn't much chance of that changing. She wasn't sure she wanted to be alone with this man. It was too tempting.

Even with as angry as she was that he hadn't emailed, that he'd spent the day on Kerri's arm, she knew she wouldn't be able to control herself. She'd give him anything he wanted.

She absolutely hated giving him that satisfaction.

Hawk sidled up closer behind her until she felt the hard muscles of his thighs pressed against her back. Running his hands up both her arms, he bent and kissed her neck.

"What do you think you're doing?" She pushed the chair away from the desk, stood and spun to face him.

He stepped back to let her, then shoved her discarded chair aside and moved in again.

With one warm, rough hand, he cupped her face. Her butt was pressed against the desk. She had nowhere to go to get away from him.

Did she really want to get away? She had to swallow the lump forming in her throat as she ached to reach out and touch the man so close to her.

"I'm picking up where we left off in Germany." He focused his gaze on her mouth as he bent slowly toward her.

Ignoring how much her lips craved his, Emily widened her eyes at the nerve of that statement. "Oh no, you're not."

"Why not? You want me as much as I want you. I can see it written all over your face."

"That's not true." Emily was one of the worst liars on earth, but she figured it was worth a shot.

Hawk grinned. "You've said that before, beautiful. Remember, back in Germany right before you jumped me?"

The reminder fought back Emily's raging hormones and brought her screeching to her senses. "You're right. I did, and you never even emailed me afterward. Oh, wait, sorry. Correction. You did email me. One damn word and then nothing. And now you're all flirty with that Kerri London."

She shoved him away hard, but a part of her immediately regretted the loss of his warmth.

Hawk narrowed his eyes and for the first time during this

encounter, he appeared unsure of himself. "No flirtier than you are with that Aussie cameraman."

"I am not."

"Bullshit."

"It is not bullshit. I do not flirt with him." Emily feared she might have actually stomped one foot like a child as she made that statement, but continued anyway. "You want to see flirting, take a look at Kerri London. *That* is flirting. I do not flirt."

"Okay, maybe you don't, but Crocodile Mel sure as hell does with you, and you're all too ready to let him, aren't you?"

"So what? I'm not involved with anyone. You have no claim on me, David Hawkins."

"No, I don't. You're right." Impossibly, he looked almost sad about that. Hawk drew in a long, slow breath. "I'm sorry I didn't email you."

An apology from Hawk. Emily had to wonder exactly how many women could claim they'd received one of those. She guessed not many.

"Why didn't you?"

He let out a short laugh. "It seemed like a good idea at the time."

Emily crossed her arms and glared at him. "Yeah, well it wasn't. In fact, I can tell you it sucked."

Don't cry, don't cry, don't cry. Emily repeated the mantra to herself. Willing her misty eyes to listen up and follow orders, she stared unfocused at the ceiling.

"I know. It was a mistake and I really am sorry." Hawk moved closer. She didn't move away.

"Why are you bothering kissing up to me? Little Miss USO was all over you today. Why don't you go be with her? I'm fairly certain you'll get lucky." *If he hadn't already.*

Hawk chuckled. "Little Miss USO. That's funny. And I'm not interested in Kerri. I'm interested in you."

Hating the hope that was beginning to sprout in her chest, she held on to the memory of a smiling Hawk attached to

Kerri London's hip. She hated it about as much as she loathed that he called her Kerri while Emily had been everything from *doll* to *Goldilocks* to *boss* on this trip.

Yet Hawk still claimed he was interested in her.

Emily let out a huff of air. "You don't show it very well."

"I'll show you now." Hawk's lips covered hers in an instant.

She couldn't fight it. Truth be told, she didn't try. As his mouth crushed hers, the tears escaped until they wet her face and crept into the kiss.

"I'm so sorry, Emily." Hawk wiped her cheek as he continued to deliver kisses between his words. "So sorry."

He lifted her like she weighed no more than a rag doll, set her on the desk's edge and stepped between her legs.

His kisses became more passion-filled and less apologetic.

Emily knew being with him again now would make leaving again in two days even harder than it had been the first time they parted in Germany. She hated that she didn't seem to care. She wanted to be with him, as painful as it would be later.

Hawk pulled back and grabbed her face in both of his hands. "I'm gonna lock the door." He stared at her, waiting.

"Okay." With a tremor in her voice, Emily answered the question he hadn't asked.

Drawing in a sharp breath, Hawk spun away. He flipped the lock and was back in the blink of an eye. Then his hands were everywhere.

Emily didn't blame Hawk for his haste. Her hands were on him too. She couldn't get enough of him.

Simply touching wasn't enough, even after he'd undone her pants and slid his hand inside her panties. She wanted his hot skin pressed against hers. Wanted him inside her.

That would be the only thing that might satisfy her need. Even then, she wouldn't stay satisfied for very long. This man haunted her.

Wasn't that always the way? The man she couldn't have was of course the one she wanted.

He pressed her back so she lay against the desk with her feet hanging off the edge. His gaze followed his hands down her body as he pushed her pants down her legs.

"Emily." He swallowed hard. There was a question evident in both his expression and his voice as he said her name—her real name.

In answer, she spread her legs and made room for him to step between them. He drew in a shuttering breath and reached for his back pocket.

Hawk covered himself with the condom he'd pulled out. Why did he have it? For her? For Kerri? Was it part of every GI's standard equipment?

He was with her, not with Kerri. That had to mean something.

She didn't find answers to her questions before he leaned low. His gaze boring into hers, Hawk slid deeply inside her.

The feel of him was so familiar, even here and now on a cold metal desk in a strange office in the middle of Afghanistan. With Hawk over her, loving her, Emily felt like she was home.

The delicate wall she'd worked so hard to construct around her bruised heart crumbled more with every thrust of Hawk's body into hers. She responded to him like they'd been made for each other . . . and in two days she'd leave him again.

Emily realized she was in big trouble when she found herself crying and coming at the same time. Her body clenched around him as the tears flowed freely.

More tenderly than a man his size and usual demeanor should have been capable of, Hawk wrapped her in his arms. He shushed her to quiet her sobs while still making love to her.

With a shudder and a groan, he came a moment after her. Still covering her body with his, he held her tighter. "You all right?"

"No." That was the truth, plain and simple.

"I am sorry." Hawk brushed a stray hair out of her face.

The act nearly melted her. She couldn't let it. He was who he was—a love 'em and leave 'em soldier whose life was the Army. A moment of gentleness didn't alter that.

"I know you are. But nothing's changed. You're going to do it again. Going to ignore me."

He shook his head. "No. I won't."

Staring up at the ceiling, Emily let out a bitter laugh. "Yes, you will. You'll go away in two days and I'll never hear from you again unless you're forced into another assignment."

"You will hear from me. You'll see." The determination in his voice almost made her believe him.

With two muscular arms, Hawk levered himself off both her and the desk. With a snap of latex, he tugged off the used condom and pushed it deep into the trashcan. After the evidence was buried beneath the discarded papers and what looked like the remnants of someone's meal, he began to button his pants.

With a sigh, she sat up and started to do the same.

His eyes never left her as she dressed. "Damn. I wish I could take you back to my tent with me."

Emily wished the same thing. If she was going to have a freshly broken heart, she might as well enjoy a full night of sex first. "We could go to my tent maybe?"

Reaching out to touch her face, he shook his head with a sad smile. "That would be very nice, but it's not a good idea. I could get in big trouble. Being in here was too damn risky as it was."

"Okay, I understand." Not really, but . . .

Hawk stepped forward and drew her close. He bent low and kissed her again. He let out a sound of near pain when he pulled away. "Ready to get back to the real world?"

Not even close. Still trembling, Emily nodded. "Sure."

Hawk looked them both over one last time, she guessed to make sure they were dressed and put back together enough to be seen in public. Then he moved toward the door.

He paused with his hand on the lock. "I'll walk you to your tent. You shouldn't be out alone this late."

Nodding, she grabbed the folder from the desk and pretended they hadn't just had sex on top of it as she followed him out the door.

CHAPTER TWENTY-FOUR

Making love to Emily was easy. Trying to get some sleep afterward knowing she was here on base so close and yet so far—not so much.

Tired and still wanting more of her, Hawk finally dragged his sorry ass out of his rack and hit the showers.

The hot water striking his back felt good. He had plans to stay under the pounding spray for a good long time . . . or at least until he felt human again.

While he stood and let the water wash away the fatigue, his mind wandered back to his too short time with Emily. His body reacted with some pretty visible results. He considered if he had the energy or the desire to deal with it now.

"Hawk! Are you in here?" Pettit's voice so close on the other side of the shower curtain deflated Hawk's excitement in no time.

"Yeah. What?" Hawk knew he sounded as exhausted and cranky as he felt.

A man couldn't even take a damn shower in peace. He'd deal with this kind of shit at the FOB where attacks came day and night, but here during a damn USO tour he should be able to relax for five minutes in the shower.

"Holy shit, Hawk. You have to get out here."

Apparently there'd be no relaxing and no more shower.

Soap still in his eyes, Hawk rinsed his face, turned off the water and slung the towel around his waist, not worried any longer he'd embarrass himself with an Emily induced hard-on.

Ready for anything but really wishing he had his gun and some clothes on, Hawk pushed out from behind the shower curtain. He came face to face with a very flustered Pettit.

"What? What's wrong?"

"It's Wally."

When it came to attracting trouble, that kid was a life-sized magnet. "Where is he?"

Hawk pulled his uniform T-shirt over his head, not taking the time to tuck the hem into the waistband of his pants.

"That's the part you aren't going to believe. He's in Kerri's tent."

"Aw, fuck." Hawk jumped on one foot as he shoved a sockless foot into his boot, grabbed his jacket in his fist and ran for the door.

He'd had a bad feeling about Wally's ability to resist that woman's overt flirting. What he'd been counting on was that Kerri was all show and she wouldn't actually follow through.

Bad call on Hawk's part, because now Wally could get into huge trouble. Looking down at his barely dressed, definitely non-regulation appearance, Hawk realized so could he if anyone saw him looking like this.

Hell of a poster boy for the US Army he'd turned out to be.

Hawk barely noticed the cold air against his wet skin as they ran through the entrance to the tent used by Kerri's entourage . . . only to be stopped by the steel wall that was her personal bodyguard blocking the way.

He heard Kerri say, "Let them through, Tony. It's okay."

Looking around the man, Hawk saw Kerri, fully clothed and wringing her hands. "I didn't know who else to call. I'm pretty sure he can get into trouble for this and I didn't want to cause that. I had Tony look for you but he could only find Ryan."

Hawk looked around the otherwise empty space and frowned. "I don't understand. Where's Wally and what happened?"

Kerri hooked a thumb at the door behind her. "In there."

That didn't explain much, but Hawk didn't require words when he could just go find out for himself. He preferred that actually—seeing things for himself.

Striding to the next room, the picture awaiting him there truly was worth a thousand words.

"Jesus, Wally."

Seeing his newly promoted sergeant stretched out face down, naked and tangled up with an equally undressed female had Hawk cursing even more colorfully beneath his breath.

Judging by the woman's uniform lying on the floor, she was with the 455th Air Expeditionary Wing of the USAF. Fraternization at its most blatant.

"Pettit, get in here. Kerri, can your guard keep everyone out of here until I clean up this mess? I mean everybody. I don't care if it's a five-star general or the president of the United States, they cannot, I repeat cannot enter this room."

"You got it, Hawk. Tony?" Kerri glanced back at her hired brute as he folded his arms and nodded, relieving Hawk's worries somewhat on that front.

Now for Wally... The scene looked like a cross between a frat-house party and a Roman orgy. The violation was enough to get Wally court-marshaled and kicked out of the service.

Hawk eyed an empty bottle of bourbon lying sideways on the floor. At least that helped to explain things.

He picked up the glass bottle and handed it to Kerri. "Civilians can probably get away with drinking on base, but Wally..." He shook his head.

Kerri got his drift and nodded, eyeing the bottle. "Gotcha. I'll be more careful with my empty Wild Turkey bottles in the future."

Stashing it deep in the garbage bin already mostly filled with water bottles and Styrofoam plates, Kerri winked at him, and Hawk said a silent thank you that she was being so cool about this.

They might just get Wally out of this mess without a trip to the brig first.

"We've got to get him up, dressed and out of here." Hawk had been thinking out loud, but Pettit stepped forward as if he'd issued an order.

Pettit grabbed a bottle of water off the floor and cracked the top. Standing over the bed, he looked a bit too pleased as he doused Wally's head with the entire contents.

It took a bit of time to bring Wally to. He started out sputtering and then looked hazily around the room through squinted eyes.

Hawk watched as the pieces began to fall into place in Wally's addled brain. He waited for full realization to set in before he bothered yelling at him.

Wally glanced down at the naked girl beneath him and there it was—the *oh shit* look.

"Wally, what the hell were you thinking?" Hawk crossed his arms and waited.

Still naked, Wally sat up on the edge of the mattress. He looked dazed as he shook his head. "Hell if I know. I guess I wasn't thinking."

"Obviously." Hawk averted his eyes with a scowl. "Can you please put some clothes on?"

Wally grabbed a pair of underwear off the ground from amid the tangle of discarded clothes, pulled them on and then sat down heavily on the edge of the bed with his forearms braced on his knees.

Airman whatever-her-name-was still didn't stir, which was probably for the better. One problem at a time.

"Oh, he was thinking all right, Hawk, but with the little head instead of the big one." Pettit grinned at his own joke.

Hawk shot him a look to silence him before he turned his attention back to Wally. "If someone besides me and Pettit found you here, you could at the very least be stripped of your new rank. You'd be damn lucky if you didn't end up out of the Army totally with a dishonorable discharge."

"I know, Hawk. I was stupid."

Hawk continued, undeterred by Wally's contrition. "And then we have to hope she doesn't press charges. You outrank her. If she decides to cry sexual harassment or worse, rape—"

"I know. I'm sorry. I swear to you. I won't let it happen again. Ever." Wally shook his head miserably.

Hawk went on, "And if she does end up talking and you lose that promotion and get busted back down to specialist or lower, you know it's going to fuck with your head. I can't, I won't, have you become a liability downrange and put my men at risk."

Wally sat looking repentant, head shaking. Hands shaking too, now that Hawk took a closer glance.

Hawk sighed. "Get dressed and get out of here."

"Yes, Staff Sergeant." Judging by his tone and the sudden switch to the formal address, Wally had realized he was in very deep shit.

Once dressed, an obviously hung over Wally slunk out of the tent after taking one last backward glance at the unconscious girl still on the bed.

Pettit watched him go. "You think he learned his lesson?"

Hawk snorted out a short laugh. "No."

"But I bet he'll at least be on his best behavior for the rest of the time we're here," Pettit offered.

Hawk sighed. "Yeah, maybe. But I can tell you one thing. I'm not going to let him forget this. When it comes time for maintenance duty back at camp, Sergeant Wallace, if he's lucky enough to still hold that rank, is going to be first on my list."

Pettit laughed. "I have no doubt, Hawk. I have no doubt."

Grabbing a twisted sheet hanging from the bottom of the bed, Hawk pulled it up, covering the naked girl the best he could without getting too close.

"What do we do with her?" Pettit asked with a glance at the Airman.

Good question.

"I guess we leave her here to sleep it off. Will you go make sure Wally keeps himself out of sight until he doesn't look and smell like he rolled in a bottle of bourbon?"

"Sure thing, Hawk." With a nod, Pettit left to do as he was told like a good soldier. If only Wally could be so obedient.

Turning, Hawk noticed Kerri hovering in the doorway. "That okay with you? If we leave her here to sleep it off?"

"Of course. It's her room while I'm here anyway. Until now she's been no problem. Real quiet girl." Kerri glanced at the figure on the bed then looked back to Hawk. "She did hint her boyfriend back home had sent her a Dear John, or I guess Dear Jane letter. That's probably what got into her, besides Wally that is." Kerri laughed at her own little joke and walked out to the front of the tent.

Hawk followed her. "Thanks for calling me. It could save his career."

Kerri smiled. "No problem."

Hawk and Emily had broken some rules themselves last night. He smothered any feelings of guilt about yelling at Wally. Yeah, Hawk had made an unwise decision, but with one big difference—Emily was a civilian, making it a shade less illegal.

They also hadn't been drunk. Nope. Alcohol wasn't required for either of them to want to jump each other at inappropriate times and places.

Hawk glanced back at the doorway to the room where the Airman still slept. "I just hope she's smart about this."

"She's a decent kid, Hawk. She's been assigned to me as kind of a liaison since I arrived. I think she'll do the right thing and keep this quiet. She will if I have anything to say about it anyway."

Hawk smiled. "You're one in a million, Kerri."

She nodded. "Yeah, I know, Hawk. Too bad I'm not the one in a million for you."

Surprised, Hawk had to laugh. "You don't want a tired, mean old soldier like me, Kerri. Believe me."

"You'd be surprised what I might want." Kerri ran one red polished nail down Hawk's T-shirt.

It did nothing for him.

Sure, she was hot. Yeah, a few months ago he may have fallen into bed right there with this woman, broken a few rules and never looked back. But things had changed and without his even realizing it.

Hawk grabbed her hand, moved her fingers from his chest and gave them a gentle squeeze. "Sorry, Kerri."

She smiled. "Whoever she is, I hope she appreciates you."

Laughing out loud, Hawk shook his head. "Nope. I can honestly say she doesn't. Not yet anyway. But one day, she will."

"She'd better. If she doesn't, give me a call. Now that this little situation has bonded you with my bodyguard, your phone call might actually make it through to me."

Hawk smiled. "I'll keep that in mind. Thanks again."

"No problem, sugar."

He pulled on the jacket he still held balled in one fist. With socks shoved in one pocket and his shirt still not tucked properly into his pants or his pants tucked into his boots, Hawk took a quick peek outside the door.

Making sure no brass was around to see him, he skirted around the side of Kerri's tent and headed for his own.

CHAPTER TWENTY-FIVE

Wally's poor judgment and the still looming possible consequences aside, Hawk still walked to the USO offices with a spring in his step.

He had more events with Kerri, the ever-present Tony and the mismatched team of photographers for another day's fun, but he also had another entire day with Emily. If he had anything to say about it, they'd also have some more private time together tonight.

He opened the door to the office and realized by the look of the full room he was the last to enter. Used to being the first to arrive most places, Hawk decided to cut himself some slack. His morning had already been fairly eventful and the day hadn't even really started yet.

Kerri, sporting an interesting outfit comprised of a camo flak jacket and black high-heel boots, was the first to greet him. "Good morning again, sugar."

"Morning." His gaze searched the room as he responded to Kerri.

Spotting Emily, Hawk started to go over when Kerri stopped him with a hand on his arm.

"Oh, Hawk. That issue you were worried about? It won't be a problem. She's so embarrassed she made me swear that I wouldn't tell anyone about it, so I think your boy is in the clear."

That got his full attention. Hawk let out a breath filled with relief. "Thanks, Kerri. That's really good to hear."

"Yeah, I thought you'd like that." Kerri grinned and then went back to sipping from her water bottle.

Hawk glanced across the room to Emily. She sat at the corner desk scribbling furiously with her head down.

Happy to find her separated from the group so they'd have some privacy, Hawk went to her. He smiled at the memories that flooded him as he passed what had become *their* desk the evening before.

"Hey, sweet thing. I missed you last night." He lowered his voice so the rest of the room's inhabitants wouldn't hear.

She raised her head and venom shot from her glare. "Don't you talk to me. Jai will be running things today as soon as I give him some instructions. Don't worry, Hawk. You won't have to see me again before you leave."

"What? Why? What's the matter?" Hawk frowned, totally and completely confused. He tried to catch her eye, to read her face, but she looked away. "Emily. Look at me."

Standing, she started toward the door. He grasped her arm. "Emily. What's the matter? Everything seemed fine last night. I thought—"

"I saw you," she hissed.

Hawk frowned. "Saw me what?"

She didn't answer, but he saw her eyes grow glassy with unshed tears combined with anger.

"Emily, you saw what?" he asked again, still clueless. "What's wr—"

A deafening blast cut off his question.

It was so strong, it rocked the ground they stood upon and he had to reach out with his free hand and grab the desk to steady himself.

"What in the bloody hell was that?" After that exclamation, the Aussie was running out the office door, video camera in hand, straight toward the undisclosed danger rather than away from it like any sane civilian would.

"Wait. Don't . . ." Hawk yelled to stop the idiot, but he was gone already.

Emily took that opportunity to wiggle from his loosened grip on her arm and make a run for the door herself.

"Emily, no!" Hawk didn't know what had exploded, but he did know he wanted Emily near him where he could protect her until he found out.

He tackled her just as she cleared the entrance of the building, taking them both down into the dirt as the many sirens scattered throughout the base erupted.

Amid the garbled loudspeaker announcements, people were running everywhere he looked.

"Get off of me." Nearly hysterical, she struggled against him, unbelievably strong for a female her size.

His attention split between the bedlam on base and the hellion beneath him, Hawk somehow managed to grab both of Emily's flailing fists in one of his hands and pin them above her head.

"Listen to me. I don't know what the hell is wrong with you. I don't have time to deal with it now. I'm a little busy trying to keep you alive. Now get the fuck back in that building or I'll put you in there myself."

He hated treating her like this, resorting to frightening her, but it was necessary. Emily stared at him with a mix of hate and fear in her tear-filled eyes.

Finally, she nodded and looked controlled enough he felt confident he could let her up and she wouldn't bolt.

He was right. She struggled to stand, refusing his hand up, brushed the dust off her pants and strode inside.

Back in the USO office, Hawk had no time to comfort Emily because chaos had broken out among their small group as well.

Hawk moved his focus to the others once Emily was safely inside. He stood stunned, deciding how to deal with this situation, just as the Aussie returned to the room.

"The east wall of the prison facility is blown to bloody bits," the breathless cameraman reported.

Hawk instinctively reached for his M16 and realized it wasn't there. All he had was his sidearm. A pistol was better than nothing, but damn, he'd give anything for Pettit, Wally and his automatic weapon right about now.

Mel stood in the center of the room and addressed the group. "We're sitting ducks if they find us here in this office with nothing but Hawkins's pistol to protect six people. I think we should make a run for it. There's a bunker not far—"

Tony shook his head, pivoting it emphatically atop his abnormally thick neck. "No way. We stay here where I can protect Kerri."

"How far is that bunker?" Jai asked over Tony.

Hawk surveyed the group—Emily an emotional mess, Kerri in spike heels, the three-hundred-pound Tony who probably hadn't run anywhere since grade-school gym class, the unarmed Aussie ready to take on the insurgents single-handedly, and one Rastafarian with a camera.

The answer to the question about the bunker's distance was obvious to Hawk—not close enough to risk it.

Knowing he had to do something to manage the situation and fast before things spiraled any more out of control, he shouted, "Listen up!"

When the room fell silent, he continued, "When we're taking pictures or up on stage, you all can be in charge. But here and now, for this situation, if you people want to stay alive and get out of here in one piece, I'm in charge. That means you do what I say quickly, calmly and without question. Do you understand?"

He looked around the room and saw a collective nod from among the assembly. The combined adrenaline felt almost palpable to Hawk's over-tuned senses.

"Now, here's what we know. Someone, most likely a guerilla faction of the Taliban, blew the wall of the base prison. I assume they did that to break out someone important to them who's being held there, and until they accomplish that goal they aren't going to leave."

"And for some even more good news," Mel piped in, "that facility with the giant hole in the wall can hold up to five hundred prisoners. Most of them Taliban or al Qaeda suspects who are not bloody happy to be here."

Great. Hawk sighed.

"But won't they just want to get the hell out of prison and run for the hills?" Kerri asked.

Mel shook his head. "We have to remember, love. These people don't care if they live or die, and they will gladly take us with them. In their opinion, the more infidels and evil occupiers—meaning us—they can kill the better."

Hawk took back control of the floor before this guy frightened them into further frenzy. "We have an undisclosed number of insurgents within the perimeter of the base who are obviously in possession of explosives and most likely weapons. We have the escaped prisoners, and I'm assuming snipers outside the fences. But we're within the largest US base in Afghanistan. The troops here are well armed and trained. They can handle this."

"So what does this all mean for us, Hawk? What do we do? Tell us what to do, sugar." Kerri's unquestioning faith in him put even more pressure on the already overwhelming situation.

Hawk had been prepared for almost every scenario in training and in battle, but he was experienced in leading a squad of skilled professional soldiers, not a laughably diverse group of untrained civilians.

"We stay here and sit tight for now." He didn't want to say it, but he didn't know what else to do without putting them all in jeopardy.

At least he had some semblance of control here. If the insurgents came through the door, he had his sidearm. He knew Tony had some firepower hidden on his person too. That made two handguns to at least defend the women with.

If their attackers chose to blow the building instead . . . Hawk decided not to think about that right now. He could only hope the baddies were more occupied with freeing the prisoners—possibly five hundred of them if the facility was at full capacity.

Shit. How the fuck did this happen?

Maybe he should risk a run for the bunker with them all.

Catching Emily's gaze, he saw hate and anger in her eyes before she looked away again. One problem at a time. He couldn't figure out what was wrong with her if he didn't keep her alive first.

"If only we had some weapons." Jai let out a breath.

Hawk shook his head to disagree. "No. Weapons in the hands of the untrained are worse than no weapons at all."

"Four years ROTC in college. One tour in the sandbox courtesy of the Army and two more years embedded as an AP photographer in Kandahar. That enough training for you?" Jai cocked one brow in his direction.

Well, damn. That's what he got for judging a book by its cover. Hawk nodded. "Yeah, it's enough, but we still don't have any weapons."

"I have a weapon, and I know how to use it," Tony said succinctly.

Just as Hawk had suspected. How Tony had smuggled that on base Hawk didn't even want to imagine.

"I know, Tony, and I'm glad for that at least. But whatever you're hiding not so effectively in that shoulder-holster under your jacket doesn't have enough range or firepower to do us much good against what those guys have out there."

"I have a phone." Emily spoke for the first time since the explosion.

"You have signal? I haven't been able to get shit out here." Tony held up his own phone.

"Satellite phone," Jai answered Tony's question for Emily.

This whole thing was too surreal, discussing cell-phone signal in the middle of an attack on a supposedly secure base.

Hawk laughed. "Well, that's great. Who are you gonna call, Emily?"

"My boss." She answered him with unmistakable attitude.

She was being deliberately evasive because she was angry

with him, for what he would love to know.

"Emily. Please. This is not the time—"

"My boss is engaged to BB Dalton. He's part of a SpecOps team." Emily interrupted his lecture.

Yeah, Hawk knew the team. "Emily, Dalton and his boys are too far away to do us any good. From the States or even Germany to here is—"

She shook her head. "No, they're not home. Katie mentioned they're at some training thing in Kabul this week. That's not too far."

Hawk could have hugged her for that piece of information, if he thought she wouldn't slug him.

He laughed. "No, that's not too far."

Hawk never thought he'd be happy to hear the name Dalton again, but in this situation he was.

Kabul to Bagram was probably about sixty kilometers. If Zeta could lay hands on a Black Hawk, which Hawk had no doubt they could, they could be there in under thirty minutes. But then what?

Seven men against an insurgent uprising and prison break—even Zeta might have trouble with those odds.

"Call her, Em. Call now," Jai said.

Emily fumbled getting the phone out of her bag. She dialed with visibly shaking hands. After a few tense moments her expression became visibly relieved. "Katie. I need you to get a hold of BB right away . . ."

The entire process probably took less than five minutes but moved in slow motion the way things often did in times of crisis. It seemed like an eternity between the time Emily had told her boss about the situation and disconnected, and when her phone rang again.

The attention of every person in the room was on her as she fumbled to pick it up.

"Hello . . . BB, thank God." Emily's voice broke on a sob.

Hawk moved to stand closer to Emily. Tears glistening in her eyes, she spoke with Dalton through the satellite phone. She nodded a few times at whatever he'd said, then she held the phone up to Hawk. "He wants to talk to you."

Taking a deep, steadying breath, Hawk pressed the phone to his ear. "Dalton, it's Hawk."

"Hawkins, am I glad you're there with Emily for this."

"Me too." More than Dalton could ever know.

The connection was bad and Dalton sounded as if he was shouting over a hell of a lot of background noise, but Hawk was happy to hear the bastard's voice.

"Listen up, Hawkins. The commander's on the line with CentCom now. I didn't tell Em this, but we've been briefed as to the conditions there. I have to be honest with you, it's not good."

No shit. "Yeah. I had kinda guessed that."

"What's your situation? Are you secure?"

"We've got nothing but two handguns among us as far as firepower. I've got five civilians holed up with me in a wood-constructed office building located in the center of the base."

Jai cleared his throat pointedly.

"One of the civilians is former military." With a glance at the photographer, Hawk amended his statement. "Another is hired muscle, so I'm pretty sure he knows his way around a gun. Two more are women and one's an Australian reporter."

"Cameraman, mate. Not a reporter, and I did some time in the Australian military myself," the Aussie corrected him.

Suddenly, it seemed everybody thought they were warriors. Hawk rolled his eyes.

He heard Dalton speaking to someone on his end of the line, then he was back. "Matt says he traced the signal from your satellite phone. He's pinpointed your precise location within the base on the GPS. Wait for us there. We're already in the air on our way to you."

So Zeta knew where they were. Great. But what the hell they thought they were going to do once they got here, Hawk couldn't even begin to guess.

"Roger that, Dalton. You got any suggestions for the meantime?"

"Just don't move from your present position until you

hear from me," Dalton instructed.

Don't move? Hawk raised a brow. All of Task Force Zeta's super secret training, all of their science fiction worthy state of the art implants and toys, and that was the best advice Dalton could give? The same plan Hawk had already settled on before the phone call.

"Great. Thanks." Hawk shook his head and began to consider a contingency plan of his own, just in case Miller's golden boys weren't as superhuman as they thought.

"I'm sorry, Hawk. I'll get back to you. We'll have more specifics soon. Keep the phone nearby. I'll call you back."

"Copy that."

Dalton disconnected the call, leaving Hawk staring down at the black object in his hand. His fingers itched for his rifle, but instead, he was forced to depend on a damn phone and Pretty Boy Dalton and the Zetas to save him.

He was not a happy man.

"What'd they say?" The Aussie had moved to stand closer.

"To sit tight."

"I'm not too good at sitting around doing nothing, mate." Mel's proclamation sounded more like a threat.

Fists clenched, Hawk sucked in a breath through his nose, trying to control his anger. "You think I am?"

Kerri stepped between the two. She turned to Hawk and laid a hand on his forearm. "Listen, sugar. We know you're doing the best you can. If whoever was on that phone told you to sit tight, then we sit tight."

Hawk heard an irritated huff come from the corner of the office where Emily had sequestered herself since handing him the phone.

What the hell had he done to deserve this?

And while he was wondering about things, where the hell was his Alpha team leader? And for that matter, Wally too? Even hung over, Wally would still be a help.

Instead, Hawk was alone to deal with one inexplicably angry and obviously jealous woman, a loose cannon cameraman and, lest he forget, an insurgent bombing and breached prison facility.

So much for his simple modeling assignment.

A camera flash brought him out of his reverie. Turning toward Rasta-photographer, Hawk frowned. "What the hell do you think you are doing?"

Camera still in hand, the man flashed brilliant, white teeth. "Recording this moment for posterity, and possibly winning me some photo awards. People love pictures of this kind of shit."

Hawk growled and was about to tell him what he thought about that when the phone rang again.

He punched the button to answer it. "Hawkins."

"Hawk, it's Dalton. Listen close. We have an ETA for our arrival. This is what I need you to do. First, do not move from that building for any reason. No matter what. Do you hear me?"

"Yeah. I heard you the first time. What's the plan?"

"Can't tell you that. This isn't a secure line. You're gonna have to trust us, Hawkins."

Trust Dalton? With Emily's life and that of four other civilians currently in his care? Not a situation Hawk wanted to be in, but it looked as if he had no other choice.

"Dalton?"

"Yeah?"

"Don't screw up or I'll have to kill you."

Hawk heard his laughter through the static on the line. "Zeta doesn't screw up, Hawk. You of all people should know that."

And if Pretty Boy thought that Hawk had forgotten they were all here in Bagram and in this mess because of that stupid bet made in a moment of insanity in the Alps, he was dead wrong. Hawk only hoped they all lived to regret the decision he'd made in those mountains some more tomorrow.

"Okay, Hawk, I have to go. I need you to get the civilians under as much cover as possible immediately. Stay away from the windows and doors and do not exit that building." Dalton shouted that warning again over the sound of the helo carrying Zeta to their rescue.

"Roger that."

"Tell Em she's gonna be fine. I'll be there in a few." A click and silence followed Dalton's last statement.

Phone still in his hand, Hawk glanced around the room at all of the people depending on him.

Commanding a group of soldiers was one thing. Hawk could be certain his orders would be followed. Now, he could only hope.

He really hated hoping.

Pushing doubts aside, Hawk sprang into action. "I need the men to pair off and each grab a desk. Move them to the back of the room away from the window."

He grabbed the end of one desk himself as Tony moved to take the other side. The two cameramen did the same with another piece of furniture.

"Everybody take cover under the desks and do not move, no matter what." He looked specifically at Emily. "Do you hear me?"

Eyes wide, she nodded and started to move just as Hawk detected the sound of Black Hawks in the air.

"Move, move, move!" he shouted, running for cover himself.

Pinning Emily beneath the leg hole of one desk with his own body, Hawk heard the helicopters open fire as the good guys—at least he really hoped it was the good guys—blasted away, taking out the insurgents keeping them all pinned down within their own base.

No wonder Pretty Boy wanted them inside. Dalton must have located the building they were being held in and targeted any hostiles nearby. Hawk shook his head at the risky maneuver.

Hitting friendlies was always a possibility in this kind of situation.

Then again, Zeta had technology no normal soldier even dreamed of. Hawk and those with him were probably safer from Dalton and his guys laying down covering fire from the sky than they were from the rest of the armed personnel trying to defend the base from the bad guys already on the inside.

As Emily trembled beneath him, Hawk tucked her head under his chin.

He mumbled against her hair, "Hell of a fucking plan, Dalton." He hoped to God it worked.

CHAPTER TWENTY-SIX

The dream was never less frightening.

Surreal noises came from outside the building. Even huddled beneath both the desk and Hawk's bulk, Emily was surrounded by horrible sounds the likes of which she'd only ever heard before in war movies.

Explosions, rapid gunfire, rockets whistling through the air followed by more explosions. All of that deafening, heart-stopping noise punctuated by the constant whir of helicopters above.

Hawk held her tight, murmuring assurances she could barely hear over the firefight outside and her own pulse pounding.

In a cold sweat and with her heart racing, she awoke with a start.

Even after all this time, months later, the recollection of those events affected her in the form of nightmares. Her memories wouldn't let her rest, day or night.

The dream always started the same. She was making her way to the USO tent to check her email just after sunrise. She caught a glimpse of Hawk, buttoning his stupid camouflage jacket while sneaking out of Kerri's tent. The realization of what must have happened between them. The feeling of nausea so strong it would have emptied her stomach if she'd taken the time to eat or drink anything that morning.

The scene usually fast-forwarded to her taking shelter beneath the desk during the melee, cradled in Hawk's arms. She hated him for what he'd done and hated herself that she couldn't bring herself to push him away.

Then she'd wake up.

Maybe she needed therapy. There was no reason for her to have the nightmares. Against all odds, everyone had been rescued unharmed.

When Emily had finally heard BB's voice outside the office door, she knew everything would be all right. Two black-clad figures had broken through the flimsy wood, yelling the entire time to Hawk and Tony not to shoot, that they were the good guys.

Emily had somehow fought her way from beneath Hawk and run at BB, crashing into him hard with a hug that would have toppled a smaller man.

In the blur of shouted instructions and running that followed, before she could even begin to grasp what had happened, Emily found herself thrust into a helicopter and in the air, flying away from the battle.

While the other Black Hawks above kept the men who'd attacked the base occupied, BB and his team had whisked Emily and the rest of their small group away, minus Hawk.

Hawk wasn't with them on the helicopter, nor did he arrive later while they waited in the relative safety of the airport in Kabul for word of the situation at Bagram.

Unfortunately, Kerri London was there, and that was enough to remind Emily exactly why she shouldn't care if Hawk lived or died.

Even more unfortunate was the fact that Emily did care what happened to Hawk. She hated that.

Glancing at her bedside clock now, she wasn't at all surprised to see it read four thirty.

Why did the stupid dream always seem to come at the same time each morning? For once, she'd like to sleep at least until five thirty. Six thirty would be even better.

With a sigh, she swung her pajama-clad legs from beneath the warmth of her sheets and stumbled blindly toward the kitchen and the coffee pot. She'd learned to set up the coffee maker the night before now that the predawn awakenings had become her norm.

Yawning, Emily flipped open her laptop on the kitchen table while the steaming brew dripped slowly into the waiting carafe.

This was another habit Emily had gotten into, checking her email immediately upon waking. She did it before work each morning during the week and obsessively all day on weekends.

Worse, she'd gotten used to receiving the usual email from Hawk. She'd come to expect to find it waiting there for her. He'd emailed her nearly every day during the past months since she'd gotten home from Afghanistan.

An impressive run considering she had never responded. Not even once.

How could she respond? She didn't know what to say. Her pride wouldn't allow her to admit to him that he'd torn out her heart by spending the night with Kerri. She certainly couldn't say she forgave him, because she didn't. Yet she still anticipated the correspondence daily.

He'd long since stopped begging her to tell him what had upset her that day back in Bagram—as if he didn't know. Now he simply told her about his day—the weather, funny things Wally or Pettit had said or done, apologizing profusely when a mission or an internet outage kept him from emailing her for any length of time.

Each day she would read the email about twenty times and then save it in a special file to read again later.

Pitiful. That was the only word she could think of to describe this long-distance, one-sided, dead-end relationship with him. Just plain sad.

Emily rubbed her face hard with both hands, then focused her sleepy, bleary eyes on her email inbox.

Frowning, she noticed that there wasn't anything new from Hawk.

Fighting the disappointment, she left the other twenty or so emails from friends, family and spammers unopened and went to the cupboard to grab a coffee mug, making excuses for the lack of word from Hawk the entire way.

She'd read online yesterday that there were bad rainstorms in Afghanistan. That must be it. No internet because of the weather.

Pouring the aromatic liquid into a large ceramic cup, Emily assured herself that tomorrow, the next day at the latest, she would find an explanation and an apology from Hawk. That she'd obviously become addicted to hearing from him every day was not at all reassuring.

With a sigh, Emily carried her coffee into the bathroom. She might as well shower and get ready for the big day. Emily let out a short laugh at that thought.

It was the day of Katie and BB's wedding.

At least Katie got to have a big day. Emily had started to doubt she ever would. Certainly not with Hawk. Most likely not at all if she didn't get over her obsession with him and move on.

She grabbed her new navy blue dress and hung it behind the bathroom door so any wrinkles would steam out while she showered.

Emily shot the offending item of clothing a dirty look as envy overwhelmed her. While she wore her stupid blue dress today, Katie would be in a long white dress.

Okay, so as pregnant as she was, Katie wouldn't be wearing a traditional white wedding dress with train and veil, but it was still a wedding dress. Katie would no doubt look beautiful in the champagne-colored, simple, chic dress. It totally suited her personality and the high empire waist accommodated her rapidly growing baby bump.

Of course Emily was happy for her friends, but she still couldn't fight the depression she felt.

Hawk was a dirty rotten bastard who had slept with

another woman the same night he'd made love to her. So why couldn't Emily stop her heart from clenching each time she thought of him?

If she didn't feel so miserable all the time, she'd think she was in love with him, further proof of how pitiful she was.

What had started many months ago as physical attraction and perhaps infatuation had grown into something more as she read his words in her apartment each day.

Emily shook her head. If this was love, it sucked. Perhaps she was better off without it. She was definitely better off without him. If only she could learn to actually be without him.

That would never happen as long as she used his daily emails as a crutch. But the thought of never hearing from him again sent her into a heart-racing panic attack.

With her head beginning to ache from lack of sleep and too much thinking, Emily stepped beneath the stream of hot water. Hopefully it would wash away her bad mood as well as all thoughts of Hawk so she'd be able to enjoy Katie and BB's special day.

Emily needed to have her wits about her today, because after the nearly two-hour train ride to upstate New York, Emily would be serving as Katie's maid of honor. With all of BB's siblings and his team there, Emily alone would be representing Katie's side.

BB may have won the battle to have the ceremony and luncheon afterward in his hometown in New York with his massive family and his best friends from Zeta in attendance, but Katie had still managed to brutally cut down the guest list to a few dozen.

Maybe from among those there, Emily would meet a nice single man who would steal her heart and make her forget all about David Hawkins.

Not likely, but she could hope.

CHAPTER TWENTY-SEVEN

Hawk listened, uncomfortable as his first sergeant praised his heroism before pinning the medal on his chest. A frigging medal for saving the lives of five civilians during the Bagram bombing.

The problem was, Hawk hadn't done anything. Pretty Boy Dalton and his Zeta boys had ridden in to the rescue. The most Hawk had done was relay Dalton's damn instructions from over Emily's satellite phone and then watch helplessly as they whisked Emily and the others away in the waiting helo.

Having to watch another man rescue his girl. Talk about feeling impotent.

The only good thing about Zeta's dramatic rescue had been that with Emily on her way to safety, Hawk was free to run to his tent and grab his weapon. It had felt damn good to finally have the M16 in his hands and be doing something, anything, besides just sitting there.

He'd found Pettit and Wally in the nearest bunker and another piece of his scrambled world settled back into place.

The Black Hawk attack had done much to rattle the insurgents within the perimeter. It hadn't taken long before they were all either captured or had fled.

Hawk had helped when and where he could, always wondering about Emily's location and wellbeing until he'd finally pinned down someone affiliated with the USO who could give him confirmation she was safe.

And that was the last he'd heard about her. Not one more word in months.

That was no fault of his, because he emailed her every damn day. She never once responded, but he did it anyway. Every day, he held on to some small hope that there would be a response from her. Every day, he found instead disappointment.

He finally realized exactly how she had felt when he hadn't contacted her after Germany.

He'd screwed up once, but he wouldn't do it again. So he wrote every day he could. He would continue to do so until she changed her mind or he got shipped home and could see her again in person and change her mind for her.

"You don't look as happy as I thought you would, Sergeant. Something wrong?" His first sergeant draped his arm around Hawk's shoulders like they were old drinking buddies.

"This is just all a bit unexpected." Not to mention undeserved.

His commander laughed. "Most good things in life are, Sergeant."

Like meeting Emily had been.

How the hell he had managed to screw it up so badly and so suddenly, Hawk still didn't know. Being able to do nothing about it besides cool his heels for the remainder of his deployment might possibly drive him insane.

The sound of a helo in the distance captured Hawk's attention. Tensing, he frowned. It sounded like Lou's chopper, but he wasn't due in anytime soon.

He squinted at the horizon until it came into view. "Could that be mail call already? Seems like we just got it."

His first sergeant laughed. "You looking a gift horse in the mouth? Mail call and supplies can't come often enough as far as I'm concerned."

Hawk smiled. "Yeah, guess so."

Lou swooped in fast and dropped the chopper in a messy landing. He came running across the camp straight toward them.

Hawk's smile faded as instinct kicked in. "Something's wrong."

Taking off in a jog that turned into a full-out run, Hawk met the old man not far from where he'd landed.

"Lou. What's the matter?"

Wheezing with what sounded like it could be his last breath, Lou gasped. "Satellite's down. Couldn't get word to you. I came to get you." The breathless man shoved papers into Hawk's hand.

He looked down and saw the American Red Cross logo on the letterhead and his heart stopped. Am Cross orders only came through when family was dying or dead and the soldier needed to get home fast. And these orders had his name on them.

Hawk was anxious to get back to the States, but not like this. He tore into the envelope and skimmed down the page. He saw his sister's name and his stomach twisted. She was the only family he had left in the world.

The first sergeant was next to him in an instant. "What's wrong?"

"My sister." Hawk looked up, still in shock. "I have to get home."

He knew that he had to move, had things to do, but he couldn't seem to function. It seemed as if his brain had stopped working.

His commander took hold of Hawk's shoulders and physically turned him back toward camp. "Go. Throw what you'll need in a duffle and get on that helo."

CHAPTER TWENTY-EIGHT

"Hey there, Emmie."

Emily glanced up from her desk as a familiar Australian voice from months past filled the room.

In the doorway to her office stood the cameraman. Mel looked different, and pretty good actually, without the head-to-toe body armor and camouflage he'd worn in Bagram. He cleaned up good in boots, jeans and a white button-down shirt that set off his tanned skin.

"Mel. What are you doing here?"

"I was in New York for a job. Jai and I met up and he suggested I stop by and see you."

She was hit with a wave of nostalgia. Mel reminded her of Afghanistan and the last time she'd seen Hawk.

"So how you been, love?"

Emily shrugged. "Okay, I guess. Keeping busy."

Mel took a step closer and propped his jean-clad butt on the edge of her desk. "Jai told me you still have dreams about the bombing."

Emily scowled. "So much for confiding in Jai."

"Don't be like that, Emmie. He and I have been through it ourselves enough to know what you're feeling. He's just concerned about you."

"I guess." She sighed.

"Well, if you need to talk . . ." Mel dropped a business card on her desk. "If I'm in the country, I'll come running. If not, there's always the phone or email."

She smiled. "Thanks."

"And if you wanted to give me a call to go out, I'd like that too," Mel continued, golden eyes twinkling as he smiled at her.

Emily looked up at him with surprise. "Like on a date?"

He laughed and nodded. "Unless you're still with Hawkins."

Now it was Emily's turn to laugh. "I don't know what I am."

"If a woman isn't sure if she's with a man or not, that's invitation enough for me." Mel sobered and laid a hand over hers. "What's wrong, Emmie? Someone as pretty as you shouldn't look so sad."

Mel read her too easily, and he already knew she'd slept with Hawk, so what the heck. Emily could use someone to talk to at the moment.

She let out a sigh. "The morning of the attack I saw Hawk coming out of Kerri London's tent half-dressed. Mel, he must have slept with her . . ." She left the rest of the horrible truth unspoken. That he'd been with Kerri right after he'd been with her.

Mel looked surprised. "He didn't tell you? Maybe not since it happened right before the bombing."

"What happened right before the bombing?" Emily sat up straighter in her chair.

"Pettit found Wally plonked, starkers and arse over tit with the Air Force Sheila assigned to Kerri London. Pettit ran and got Hawk out of the shower that morning and brought him to Kerri London's tent."

Emily's heart began to pound. She didn't understand half of what he had just said, but she grasped enough to know it was important. "Mel. Please, for God's sake, could you speak English this once and tell me what happened again?"

"Sure." Mel grinned. "Wally was in Kerri's tent naked and

drunk with her liaison. Sex on base with a woman he outranked could get Wally in huge trouble. So Pettit ran and pulled Hawk out of the shower. That's why Hawk was coming out of Kerri's tent early in the morning half-dressed. He was trying to keep Wally from getting court marshaled."

That she understood and it was wonderful.

Wonderful and horrible at the same time. She'd ignored Hawk's emails for months because she'd made the wrong assumption. She'd tortured both him and herself rather than just ask him.

"Mel, you know all this for a fact?"

"Abso-bloody-lutely."

"I'll take that as a yes."

He nodded. "It's a yes. Wally told me himself after I found him emptying his guts on the ground outside my tent. Pettit backed up the story. So there's no need for you to worry."

Emily could barely listen to Mel anymore. Her mind was already on Hawk. She had to email him, but she hadn't heard from him in two weeks. What if she'd lost him? If only she could see him. If he was back in Germany maybe she could fly there, but Afghanistan . . .

Then another thought hit her. "I haven't gotten an email from him in two weeks. What if something happened there to him? Can you use your connections and check?"

He frowned. "Didn't you know? He's here."

"What do you mean he's here? Is that some sort of slang again?" She didn't dare hope.

"No. I mean he's here in the States. Emergency leave. He told me his sister was in the hospital. He got sent home to be with her since she's his only living relative."

Emily frowned. "How do you know this?"

"He flew home through Kandahar. I saw him there when he was waiting for a flight out."

A frantic feeling hit her. She had to get a message to Hawk that she was sorry before it was too late.

"I need to get on my computer. I have to look up his sister and get an address or a phone number. I have to find out where she lives."

Shit, what if his sister was married and had a different last name? Even if she wasn't married, how many women named Hawkins were there in the United States? She didn't even know his sister's first name.

It was impossible. She'd never find her. Emily's head was spinning.

"I'll have to call Katie. Maybe she can use her military connections. But she just had the baby and it's still early. I don't want to wake her."

Mel held up a hand. "Why don't you let me see what I can do?"

Shaken and desperate, Emily nodded. She was willing to try anything.

Mel whipped out a cell phone that looked nearly as big and complicated as her laptop and punched a few buttons. He rose and walked closer to the door to speak. Curious, Emily had to fight the urge to follow him and listen.

When a few minutes later she saw him take out a small notepad and pen, she nearly jumped from her seat.

Finally, Mel came back to her desk holding a piece of paper.

"Is that—"

"His sister's address and phone number."

"How did you get it?"

"Connections." He grinned.

Finally, Emily got up the nerve and grabbed the paper he held out for her.

"Pennsylvania?" she read.

Hawk was in Pennsylvania. So close. Only one state away. "But what if he's not still there?"

Mel shrugged. "I saw him a little less than two weeks ago. They wouldn't send him back so soon. Not counting travel time, which can take days each way, they usually give them at least a solid two weeks at home for emergency leave."

Emily's hopes surged. "But wait. What if his sister is really ill? Or worse, dead? I can't bust into her home looking for him while he's grieving. Can I? Then again, maybe he needs me now if she did—"

"Emmie, dial the bloody number or I'll do it for you."

Glancing at Mel, she predicted he would do exactly that. She took out her cell phone and dialed the number. She noticed her hands were shaking.

"Hello," a female voice answered the phone.

"Um, hi. I hate to bother you. I was actually looking for David Hawkins. I was told he might be there."

"Can I ask who's calling?"

"Um, it's Emily Price. I worked with him, not in the Army, but he did a job for my marketing company—"

"Of course. Emily. He mentioned you. I have to say, it's a pleasure to meet you, even if it is only on the phone. You're the first woman in thirty years that I've ever seen throw my brother off balance."

Emily swallowed hard. "Me? Are you sure he was talking about me?"

Hawk's sister laughed. "Yeah, pretty sure. But I'm sorry to tell you, David's gone already."

Her heart fell. "He is?"

"He had to get back."

"Oh. Okay. Thanks. And I hope you feel better."

"Emily, wait. He doesn't have a cell phone when he's deployed, but he checks in with me every day. Give me your number and I'll pass it along to him."

"Okay. I'll give you my home and cell numbers. And my work number too."

What if he was too mad at her to call? It didn't matter. Emily had to take a shot.

CHAPTER TWENTY-NINE

Not having a cell phone had never bothered Hawk while he was in Afghanistan, or even in Germany. But while in New York City trying to find Emily and having to check in with his sister a couple of times a day, it really sucked.

He had pretty much memorized his phone card number and was very familiar with every working pay phone en route. And now, leaning against the tiny metal shelf, pen and scrap of paper in hand, Hawk made his third phone call in the last hour. First had been to call his captain to ask him to contact Hank Miller and get Dalton's number.

Then the call back to his captain to get the info he'd obtained from Miller. Armed with Dalton's number, he was on his hopefully final call before the only one he wanted to make—to Emily.

"I don't know about this, Hawkins. I don't feel comfortable giving Emily's information out. I mean, she never even told me you two had a history together."

After all Hawk had gone through, Pretty Boy had the nerve to question his intentions toward Emily like he was her damn father. "Well, we do."

"Maybe as far as you're concerned. But Emily—"

Hawk took a deep breath to steady his temper. "Look, Dalton. I've still got more than half of my time left to serve in

Afghanistan. I'm here in the States for another two days and then I'm gone again. But I'll be back as soon as Uncle Sam lets me. I'm not looking for a one-night stand."

If Emily still wanted him, that is. Actually, fuck that. Even if she didn't, he wouldn't leave her alone until he changed her mind.

Dalton remained silent. Hawk was about to give up on this call. He could try to find a computer to email her.

He decided to give it one more try with Dalton first. "I want to build a future with her, but first I need to know where to find her."

Dalton sighed. "All right. Got a pen?"

Thank God, he'd finally given in. "Yeah. Shoot." Hawk scribbled the info Dalton relayed. "Um, I wouldn't mind knowing how big a battle this is going to be either. I mean, do you know if she's seeing someone else?"

Shit, that could be why she hadn't responded to any of his emails.

Dalton laughed. "You're really pushing it, Hawk. Fine, I don't think I am spilling any secrets if I tell you she attended my wedding alone. She was invited with a date but she chose not to bring one."

Hawk would take anything he could get. His hope renewed, he was totally sincere when he said, "Thanks, Dalton."

"You're welcome. But I have to tell you one thing."

"What's that?"

"Emily is like my sister. You hurt her and I'm going to have to do something about it."

Hawk laughed, figuring that if they really wanted to, Pretty Boy and the Zetas could probably do all sorts of things to him and get away with it. Luckily, they seemed like a peaceable group, when not dealing with insurgents, that was.

"I hear you, Dalton. I'd never willingly hurt her." Although, somehow, someway, he'd managed to do something that had upset her enough she'd frozen him out of her life.

Now that he was here, he fully intended to find out what and fix it.

Hawk wasn't all that familiar with Manhattan, but if he could find his way through the mountain paths of Afghanistan while being shot at, he figured he could navigate New York City. The streets were numbered after all.

One quick question to a passing man in a suit and Hawk knew which direction Madison Avenue was. He had no problem finding the address Dalton had given him for Emily's office building. Soon he stood in front of it, his heart pounding at the thought of seeing Emily again.

This whole trip could be a waste of time. Then again, it might not be. Determined, he pushed through the glass doors and into the lobby.

A quick elevator trip upstairs and he was walking through the office door, shaking but determined. Then there stood Emily, right in front of him and holding an obviously newborn baby.

Holy shit.

The first thought that assaulted Hawk, that nearly took him down to his knees, was that he'd gotten Emily pregnant that first time they'd had sex in Germany. But wait. That wasn't nine months ago and they'd used protection.

The second thought was that Emily having a baby was one piece of information Dalton could have let him know about during that phone call.

Had she been pregnant with another man's child both times they'd been together? She hadn't looked it in Afghanistan, but it would explain why she wouldn't email him back.

It must have been obvious to Emily by his expression that he was counting backward and trying to reason this out. Once the look of shock that had appeared when she saw him standing in the doorway finally left Emily's face, she shook her head.

"Don't worry. This is Katie and BB's baby. Not mine. Or yours."

He itched to tell her when he thought about having kids the only woman he could picture having them with was her.

Instead, he took a step forward and peeked at the infant's face. "Pretty little thing. She looks like her father."

"*He* looks like his father. It's a boy."

Hawk raised one eyebrow. "That figures." Even Dalton's son was pretty.

Emily walked to some sort of stroller thing, gently laid the baby down, covered him with a pale blue blanket and jingled some plastic colored toys that hung in front of his face. When she returned to Hawk, she looked uncomfortable.

"So I guess your sister told you I called."

"My sister?" He shook his head. "I haven't spoken to my sister yet today."

"Then how did you know where I work?"

"I tracked down Dalton and asked where to find you. I figured he owed me one."

Before she could respond to that, two men and a red-headed female came out of a back room.

The woman arched one eyebrow in surprise when she saw him. "Sergeant Hawkins. A pleasure to finally meet you." She stepped forward and extended her hand. "Katie Dalton."

"My boss," Emily added.

And Dalton's wife. Well, hell. Hawk didn't realize Pretty Boy had it in him to choose a mature, sexy businesswoman for a wife. He'd pictured him more with some model-type bimbo.

"Hawk. Our Army man. Of course, I didn't recognize you in civilian clothing." The older of the two men moved forward, one beefy arm extended.

"These are the owners of the agency. That's James Howard and his partner, Morris Dean." Emily made the introductions.

Hawk shook hands with both men as the thinner of the two, Morris Dean, asked, "What brings you to our neck of the woods? Or more accurately, to the concrete jungle of New York?"

No use lying about it. "I came to see Emily."

Dalton's wife looked very interested as she glanced from Hawk to Emily and back. "Well, it's good to meet you. Em, why don't you take the rest of the afternoon to show our new star around the city."

"Good idea. In fact, take him down to Times Square and stand him in front of that billboard with his ad on it. That should raise some public interest, don't you think?" James Howard asked his partner.

The other man bobbed his head in agreement. "Definitely. Great idea, Jim. A shame he's not in uniform, but the tourists might still recognize him. Do you need the company limo, Emily?"

Emily looked shocked by the offer. "Um. No, thanks, I think we'll be fine. It's a nice day. I'll just grab my jacket."

Just outside the office door, as they waited in awkward silence for the elevator to arrive, Hawk turned to Emily. "I might have enjoyed the limo."

Looking miserable, she ignored his joke. "Hawk, we need to talk. There's something I need to say."

He wasn't sure if that was good news or bad news. Talking was better than not, he supposed, unless of course what she had to say was leave her alone or she'd get a restraining order.

"Okay. Is there someplace we can go for some privacy?" he asked.

Times Square in front of his billboard wasn't where he wanted to be for this ominous conversation—and no one had told him he'd be on a frigging billboard anyway.

"Privacy is pretty hard to find here in Manhattan." Her throat worked as she swallowed and glanced up at him. "But my apartment isn't too far."

Her apartment. Damn, he wanted her so badly he could barely stand it.

"Okay. Let's go to your place then . . . if you don't mind." Hawk held his breath and waited.

"No. It's fine. It's even clean. I've, uh, been waking up early lately so I clean before work."

They both remained mostly silent during the cab ride to her apartment, making the trip seem eternally long. When they finally arrived, she fumbled with her key in the lock.

She walked through the door, turned to him and began speaking at the same moment he did.

"Hawk. I'm so sorry—"

"Emily, I don't know what I did, but—" Hawk stopped his apology when he realized she was apologizing to him. "Wait. What are you sorry about?"

She took a deep breath and glanced into the tiny living room. "Can we sit?"

They could stand on their heads for all he cared, as long as she was finally ready to discuss the two of them.

Hawk wanted to clear the air, the sooner the better. He'd been through too many days and nights of agony already. "Okay. Let's sit."

They moved farther into the room and he dropped his duffle to the floor. It was strange getting a glimpse into her world. Until now, she'd been on his turf. Her laughably tiny city apartment felt as foreign to him as Afghanistan probably had to her.

Seated on the couch that barely fit the two of them, Emily angled her body toward his. "I made an assumption, an incorrect assumption it turns out. I should have confronted you about it right away. Instead, I acted like a child not emailing you back."

"I don't understand. What assumption?"

"I saw you coming out of Kerri London's tent the morning of the bombing at Bagram. I assumed you'd—"

"Had sex with her? Right after I'd been with you?" Hawk sat in shock. "Emily. What the hell kind of man do you think I am?"

"It was barely dawn. You were half dressed. I—" Her eyes filled with tears. "I know. I was wrong. I'm so sorry. It's just, I was so hurt."

Hawk let out a frustrated breath as he gathered her against him. She came willingly into his arms. "You were hurting over nothing. I can't believe you spent all this time thinking I would do that to you when all you had to do was ask me."

"I would have said something that morning, but then there was the explosion."

He remembered. She had started to say something and then all hell had broken loose. Shaking his head, he squeezed her closer. All those months of agony on both their parts.

"I was getting one of my men out of Kerri's tent. That's all."

"I know. Mel told me when I saw him."

"Mel?" That name rang a bell. Hawk froze as he put the name with the man. "Crocodile Cameraman?"

Emily nodded, laughing tearfully at the nickname. "Yeah."

How the fuck could he be here in New York? Hawk had just seen him when he flew out to get home to his sister.

"So you saw Mel?" The ugly green monster inside Hawk reared its ugly head.

"This morning. He was meeting Jai and stopped by to say hello."

Who the fuck was Jai? Then Hawk remembered Rasta-photographer.

"He told me he'd seen you, then he told me about you having to get Wally out of Kerri's tent."

Hawk frowned. "So do you see this Mel often?"

Emily pulled back and looked at him. "You're jealous."

"No." Hawk sighed then opted for the truth. He'd do anything, even admit this, if it would keep Emily in his life. "Yes. I've never been so jealous of any man in my entire life."

Of course, he'd probably never felt as much for any woman as the way he did about Emily. "He was all over you in Bagram, Emily."

Emily smiled. "It was an act to make you jealous."

"You were doing it on purpose?"

"Not really." She shrugged. "It was all Mel's doing, but I kind of went along with it."

Relief overwhelmed him, along with curiosity. Although he suspected he knew the answer to his next question.

"Why?"

"Because I was jealous of you being with that flirty Kerri London every second of the day."

That was what he had hoped. Hawk laughed and pulled her closer again. "We make a hell of a pair."

They could maybe even be happy if they both stopped getting in their own way.

Emily looked up at him with baby blues that could melt a man. She leaned in. "Kiss me?"

With a groan, he tangled his hand in her hair. "You don't have to ask me twice."

Hawk crashed his mouth into hers. He'd intended to be gentle, but the pent-up passion of the past months without her rose to the surface. It poured into his kiss as he angled his head and thrust his tongue against hers. He'd needed her so badly and for so long.

They had to make enough memories to hold him for the rest of his deployment.

Wanting nothing between them, Hawk tugged at Emily's clothes. She had far too much on. He peeled off layer after layer. Suit jacket, shoes, pants and blouse. He revealed her inch-by-inch until she was in nothing but bits of lace covering the key areas he was anxious to get to.

He needed her more with each new exposed portion of her creamy skin. Hawk slid his hands over her body, her curves both familiar and new to him at the same time.

They'd only been together twice, once for the night, and once for just a few stolen moments, but he'd remember both times forever. And now she was here and it was time to create new memories.

Tasting her, caressing her, kissing her warm soft flesh was better than any of his dreams.

Her lips had never tasted sweeter, her body had never felt more responsive than at this moment.

This time seemed to be so much more than the other times they'd been together. Perhaps because he felt so much more for her now. He'd almost lost her because he hadn't let her know just how he felt. How deep his feelings for her ran. He'd never make that mistake again. This time he'd leave her with no doubt of how much she meant to him, how much he needed her.

But now wasn't the time to talk. Not when his mouth had so many better things to do.

After a struggle to get out of his jeans and button-down shirt, Hawk finally freed himself. He pulled a nearly naked Emily onto his lap.

She straddled him, facing him so he had access to everything he craved. He pushed aside the white lace of her bra and drew one taut, pink nipple into his mouth. She trembled above him.

Slipping his hand into her panties, he found her wet from wanting him. That knowledge drew a groan from deep inside him.

Burying his face against her as he took in her warm scent, Hawk pushed aside her panties and slid his fingers inside her. The feeling of her heat almost mind-blowing, he plunged into her again and again.

She rocked against his hand as he worked her clit, shaking, gasping, making those tiny noises that drove him insane as she came closer to release.

Thank God, he'd been bold enough to bring a condom, just in case she forgave him and this happened.

Stretching until he nearly fell off the couch with her in his lap, he reached his pants and got the packet. He covered himself and then guided Emily over him.

He slid in easily. They were both more than ready for this. She rode him until he felt the muscles inside her gripping him so tightly he thought he'd lose his mind.

As he felt her orgasm breaking, he thrust her down onto his cock one last time as he exploded inside her.

Still breathless, he shook his head. "I'll last longer next time. I swear. It's just . . . it's been a while."

"I'm glad to hear that."

"Which part?"

"Both." She smiled. Then the smile faded. "When do you have to leave?"

"Two days." *Too soon.*

"Are you going back to your sister's tonight?"

"Nope. But I'll have to find someplace to stay. Maybe a hotel or something." He grinned, knowing what she'd say.

Her eyes opened wide. "You will not. You're staying here."

"I was hoping you'd say that." He leaned in for another taste of her mouth, then a thought hit him. "Wait. You said you called my sister? How? She still goes by her ex-husband's last name."

She smiled. "Mel. He got her number somehow."

Hawk cocked up a brow. "Oh really."

Mel's involvement in their reconciliation didn't make him happy, but that Emily had been trying to reach him sure did. All at the same time that he was trying to get to her through Dalton.

He kissed Emily, claiming her mouth with enough force she'd forget all about Mel and everything else.

When he finally pulled back, he had only one question. "So when I get back to the FOB and I email you, you going to email back?"

She grabbed his face in her hands. "So often you're going to get sick of me."

"Not gonna happen." Hawk shook his head. "I'll never get sick of you."

Teary-eyed, Emily smiled. "Good."

So many twists of fate had brought them together, all the way back to that first day on the mountain in the Alps.

It was like the universe was telling them, over and over again, they were meant to be together. For once, Hawk was going to listen. .

BB DALTON

A Red Hot & Blue Bonus Read

CHAPTER ONE

December 2006

"Dalton!"

BB sat up a little straighter at the sound of his name being barked from the doorway by his commander.

"In my office. Now."

"Yes, sir."

Oh, shit. What the hell had he done to get called into the commander's office right before a team meeting? There was no way this could be good.

He'd arrived on time for the zero-eight-hundred meeting.

In fact, he hadn't even been the last one in the door. That honor belonged to his teammate Jack Gordon who looked as if he'd just rolled out of bed.

BB tried to ignore the raised eyebrows and interested looks of the other guys as he stood and made his way into the commander's office.

Damn it. It just figured he'd somehow get into trouble right before his leave started. He was supposed to go home to see his family in New York for the holidays. As he walked into the commander's office, feeling very confused, he hoped he'd still be waking up Christmas morning in his old bed.

The fact that he found a woman sitting in the chair opposite the commander only compounded his confusion.

If he'd been one of the guys on base who hung out at the

local bar until they had to crawl home, he might wonder if he'd had the pleasure of this woman's company, perhaps gotten a little wild and then forgotten about it and now was in trouble for it.

But he wasn't that kind of guy. It was a rare day he even drank alcohol.

He thought for a moment.

His last drink, and it was only one, had been to celebrate the return of Jack's brother Jimmy to active duty after he'd been worked over pretty bad after his cover had been blown on an undercover assignment.

That was months ago.

Besides, this woman looked less like a barfly and more like said barfly's lawyer.

He stood at attention and waited until the commander indicated he should sit in the other chair.

BB evaluated his commander's mood. Not good, but he'd seen worse.

It was almost an amused annoyance that came across in the commander's voice as he continued, "CentCom . . ."

Uh, oh. That was never a good start to a sentence. The commander hated Central Command.

". . . has decided to begin recruiting its special operatives from the civilian sector."

BB raised an eyebrow. He himself had been a Navy SEAL when he'd been recruited for one of the special task forces. These units were comprised of the best of the best from all branches of the military. But civilians?

The commander sent a paper sailing across the desk at him. "Read."

It was an NBC News article dated earlier that year. It looked like it had been printed off the internet. The headline read, *"Navy SEALs: Demand for specialized units grow."*

He silently read on.

"Navy SEALs, counted among the best commando forces in the world, are at the forefront of the Pentagon's war on terror as modern warfare continues to evolve . . ."

Nothing BB didn't already know. He skimmed down farther.

"In the next several years, the Pentagon wants to add nearly 400 more to the approximately 2,600 SEALs now in service. But with a 60 percent dropout rate, the SEALs have had to turn to a more efficient method of identifying and recruiting potentially successful recruits. As befitting an unconventional fighting force, the SEALs have come up with a creative recruitment tactic looking beyond the Navy for potential recruits. It sends SEAL mentors to high schools, air shows and sporting events to seek out candidates."

BB read, amazed. He skimmed the rest and learned they'd even sent a SEAL to compete in an Ironman Triathlon in Hawaii to recruit from among the athletes.

At least now he knew what was up the commander's butt. What he didn't get was how it involved him.

Yeah, he was in excellent physical condition, but so were the other guys. And each one had their own special skills that had led to their recruitment.

Matt Coleman was a computer genius. Trey Williams was a language expert. Jimmy Gordon was a sharpshooter. Jimmy's brother, Jack, had choirboy looks and charm, but was lethal in hand-to-hand combat. Bull Ford had his sheer size, on top of being an explosives expert.

BB was the superior swimmer and deep-sea diver on the team. He sincerely hoped he wasn't already signed up for any damned triathlon, although he wouldn't mind an all expenses paid trip to Hawaii.

He wondered what the woman present had to do with all of this. She had sat there in complete silence while he read.

Taking a minute, he glanced at her now. She was cute. No, he couldn't exactly say that. Cute was a good word to describe cheerleaders and prom queens. This woman was beautiful, with cool, sophisticated, self-assured, polished good looks.

Her brown hair was pulled back in a severe bun in the back. The fluorescent lights added red highlights to the top of her head. He'd like to see that hair down. He bet she'd look smoking hot.

She was probably a few years older than him, but that didn't stop him from glancing at the rest of her to take in her short skirt, high heels, and tight little tank top exposing some nice cleavage beneath the suit jacket she wore.

Warm brown eyes, with obvious intelligence behind them, completed the look of aloof sexiness.

Nothing wrong with a woman who could make a business suit look that good.

BB remembered the commander and glanced up. "Sir, I still don't understand."

"Dalton. You've read the fuc—um, damned article?"

"Yes, sir." BB could see the commander was editing his usually more than colorful language because of the female guest in the office.

"Well, I'm so happy to be the one to inform you that you have been selected as the new SpecOps recruitment poster boy." The sarcasm practically dripped from each word the commander spoke.

"Poster boy?"

The commander let out a bitter laugh. He was obviously not happy with Central Command.

"Yeah. I'll let Ms. Katherine Jorgenson here have the honor of explaining it to you. By the way, she's your 'handler'." The commander actually used air-quotes around the word.

Handler. BB'd had handlers before. People dedicated to making sure that *the talent* was happy. They were glorified babysitters really. That had been in another life, in another lifetime. He'd left that life far behind.

He turned to her now, wondering if there was any way to get out of this even though he didn't yet know what *this* was.

Ms. Jorgenson extended her hand to him in a very business-like manner. "May I call you William?"

Not even his mother called him William. "At home they call me Billy Bob, but the guys here call me BB, ma'am."

She seemed to wince, but then nodded. "BB, then. Please,

feel free to call me Katie rather than ma'am, since we'll be spending a lot of time together."

Spending a lot of time together. Really? Well, that wouldn't be a hardship. Maybe this gig had an upside after all.

Katie continued, "When hired, I did extensive research from the military personnel database—"

"Um, excuse me a second," BB interrupted her. He swung to look at the commander. "I thought the SpecOps personnel database was classified?"

The commander snorted, but let Ms. Jorgenson—Katie— explain. "Don't worry. I've been checked front, back and sideways by the military, the FBI and Homeland Security. I've done marketing campaigns for the sitting president as well as other high profile government personalities I'm not at liberty to name. I've been retained by Uncle Sam to develop a recruiting campaign focusing on the glamour of the special operations units."

Now it was BB's turn to snort. *Glamour?* Yeah, right.

Maybe he'd take her on his next twenty-mile run and see how glamorous she thought it was with a sixty-pound pack strapped to her back.

His not-so-high opinion of her idea didn't escape her.

"It's a whole new world out there, BB. The military needs to change with the times and market itself just like any other business. The SEALs have made a good start. But I can do it so much more effectively . . . with your help."

"Why me?" he asked.

"Well, as I started to explain, when I was shown pictures of potential candidates I recognized you."

She pulled a photo out of her briefcase and handed it to him. He didn't need to look at it. He did anyway, inwardly cringed, and then handed it back to her.

The commander smiled wide, practically laughing at him. "I knew you'd modeled before joining up, Dalton. But I guess I assumed you'd been modeling actual clothes."

"It sure threw Madison Avenue for a loop when you left," Katie said to him. Then she turned to the commander. "*No one* quits being the Andre Milano underwear man. That is, until BB."

The commander was outright laughing now. He wiped a hand across his face and tried to sober up. "I'm sorry, son. I can see you're not any happier about this than I am."

"No, sir, I certainly am not." And BB had a bad feeling that he couldn't do a damn thing about it.

CHAPTER TWO

Katie shook her head at them both.

Stubborn, short sighted men. Stuck in their ways, just like her ex-husband had been. God forbid they take a step into the twenty-first century or—*gasp*—try something new.

BB was the perfect choice for this campaign. He was hot in a boy-next-door didn't-even-realize-it kind of way.

He came with modeling experience and was a real-live special operative.

He'd changed little since his modeling days, and actually, his years in the service had given him an edge that made him even sexier. Just beneath the surface of that pretty face lurked something deep, maybe even dark.

She could see the print ads now. A larger than life-sized picture of BB on the side of a midtown bus, shirtless, camouflage pants opened wide to expose the Andre Milano briefs. His green eyes smoldering. His abs glistening. Just a bit of scruff shadowing his face. A tag line that read something like, *Women love a man in uniform . . . and out of one.*

Her heart beat faster remembering the excitement when she'd first recognized BB and had come up with the idea. She'd contacted the Andre Milano executives herself that very day. They'd been willing to pay enough for BB's image to foot the bill for this entire recruiting campaign plus some.

BB DALTON - BONUS READ

The timing had been perfect, just as they were about to launch their new active men's undergarment line. *Andre Milano, proud sponsor of US Military Special Operations.* Central Command had loved saving the money. And the exposure the military was going to get out of the connection with a company the size of Andre Milano was bigger than anything she could have arranged on her own.

It was a win-win for both entities. But first she had to convince BB to go through with it. She'd never considered he wouldn't be willing. She looked from one man to the other.

"I really can't even imagine why the both of you are being so resistant to this idea." She was bordering on being rude and she didn't care.

The commander's smile had a threatening feel to it. "Oh, Ms. Jorgenson. I believe you'll convince Joe Public that being in SpecOps is glamorous. And then we'll get an influx of recruits who yesterday couldn't be bothered to get off the sofa to tie their shoelaces, but who today think they're going to sail through BUD/S and come out the other side a SEAL. But you know what? They won't. All they'll succeed in doing is to bog down the boot camps and cost the taxpayers money."

She shook her head. "You're wrong. We're going to make it the *in* thing to be in Special Operations Forces. And *that* will attract the best of the best. Star high school and college athletes will give up a chance at pro-contracts to join up. Former Olympians will run to sign on. The Kardashians of the world aren't going to lust after rappers and stars anymore. Instead, elite SOF guys will be the new *it men.*"

BB had to laugh at that. Women already lusted after military guys, without this crap marketing campaign. He could go to the bar off base on any given night and get laid if he wanted to.

The ironic thing was, it was when he'd been modeling that he couldn't get a date. Everyone had assumed he was gay. And the only women he was around, the other models, were too self-absorbed or emaciated to even get his juices flowing.

No, thank you. Time to shut this thing down. "Ma'am . . . uh, I mean Katie. May I speak with the commander privately?"

Sighing audibly she stood. "Of course." She paused in the doorway and turned back, her gaze meeting his. "The camera loves you, BB."

Unfortunately, he didn't love the camera. She gave him one last look, and then left the room through the door that led to the hallway. He spun back to face his commander. "Do I have to do this, sir? Is it a direct order?"

"Yes and yes. What's wrong, Dalton? You're going to get monetary compensation. She didn't get a chance to tell you but it pays well." He snorted. "Better than what we pay you."

"Money's not the issue." If it had been, he would still be wearing nothing but his underwear and a smile. "What about my undercover career, sir?"

"I've already considered that and it won't be a problem. If the offer had been made to Williams, let's say, it would be different. He's already gone undercover and met with a target. We couldn't plaster his picture all over the country promoting the US military. But your specialty is sneaking in and out, quick and quiet, sometimes underwater. It's not going to make a damn bit of difference if you're famous."

BB sighed.

"Smile, Dalton." The commander hooked a thumb in the direction of the door through which Katie had just exited. "That one's a real looker and she's got a schedule that has her holding your hand practically 24/7 for the next four days. And after she's done with you, you get a week leave."

"I just never thought I'd be back in that life again."

The commander got up and slapped him on the back. "Tough life, I know, Dalton. Being around beautiful women, getting your picture taken in tighty whities. The team and I will be feeling real bad for you today while we're on the obstacle course and you're flying first class to New York with your *handler*."

All right. Maybe this wasn't going to be too bad after all.

CHAPTER THREE

That morning BB had been just another member of Task Force Zeta. That afternoon, he was sitting next to his handler in business class and sipping a complimentary beverage while flying to New York.

He hadn't been on a commercial flight in a year and then it had been in back in the cheap economy class seats, not up front.

But aside from that, there was a huge difference between this aircraft, with its television screens in every seat back, and what he was most accustomed to—a military transport, which didn't even have real seats.

He glanced at Katie next to him. She'd insisted he take the aisle because his legs were longer. She obviously wasn't aware he was used to far harsher traveling conditions than this.

She was busy squinting at her laptop, so he flipped the channels on his little TV screen. He found some sitcom reruns and settled back in his seat for the short flight North Carolina to New York.

"You all right?" Katie glanced over at him.

"Sure. Why?"

"You just sighed like you had the weight of the world on your shoulders."

He hadn't realized that. "Sorry."

It was funny. He did have the weight of the world on his

shoulders when he was actively battling the terrorist threat with his team, but he loved that job. Now, eyeball deep in this meaningless marketing fluff, he was unknowingly sighing and feeling pretty miserable.

Not to mention useless. His team could be called out at any moment and he wouldn't be with them.

"I know you hate this," Katie said.

What could he say to that? Honesty was the best policy, he supposed. "You're right. I do."

She laughed. "Ah, BB. Do you know what I like about you most?"

"No." But he wouldn't mind finding out.

"It's that you're the exact opposite of every other model I've ever worked with or even met. They run toward the limelight, and you run away from it. I have a feeling that's going to be my biggest challenge with you."

The only response he could think of was, "I'm not a model."

She laughed again. Her warm genuine smile took ten years off her face. "Whatever you say. Can we go over your schedule for while we're in the Big Apple or do you want to rest now and wait until we land?"

Rest? He'd gone days with little to no sleep. It happened routinely while on missions. Although, this whole marketing thing was proving way more exhausting than any op.

"That's fine. I don't need to rest. Go ahead." He flicked off his tiny screen that made the people look two inches tall and turned his attention to Katie, which was really no hardship since she had taken off her jacket for the flight. With her wearing that tank top, it took all his self control to keep his eyes above her neckline.

"We've got a tight schedule. I hope you're up for it."

She really had no clue what his life was normally like, did she? He didn't bother to explain and just nodded. "I'll do my best."

CHAPTER FOUR

Katie watched BB as she outlined what she considered to be an aggressive schedule of appointments, press interviews, photo shoots and live appearances.

He didn't bat an eye. Any other model would have been ranting, raving and calling their agent by now to demand down time. Not BB. She wondered when he would finally stop surprising her.

"So, what do you think?" she asked when he didn't offer any comment besides a nod during her entire run-down.

He shrugged. "Fine."

She huffed out a breath. He wasn't complaining, but she could tell he wasn't happy either. "Are you really fine?"

"No, but that doesn't mean I'm going to take it out on you."

"What's the problem here, BB? Why are you so against doing this?" She'd played therapist for more than one model during her career. She could step into that role easily enough for BB now. "Talk to me."

"I don't like attention." The tone of his objection was flat. Matter of fact. And ridiculous, in her opinion.

"Then why did you become a model in the first place?"

"Because I'm the youngest of nine kids and I couldn't afford college otherwise. I wasn't super smart, so I couldn't get an academic scholarship. I was a good athlete, but not good enough to get a free ride. What I was, was good looking enough people wanted to take pictures of me." He shrugged again.

"Wouldn't the military have paid for your tuition?" she asked.

"I started modeling the summer before my senior year of high school, long before I knew I wanted to enlist. The ironic thing is, once I started modeling full time, I didn't have time for college. I took a couple of night classes and never got my degree."

"What made you realize you did want to enlist?" She was getting personal, but she was too fascinated by this glimpse into his past to stop digging deeper.

"I was in the city for a photo shoot on September eleventh. I watched the first tower fall. I finished up my contract obligations and enlisted the day after."

Wow. That she hadn't expected.

"You joined up, knowing almost for certain we'd be heading into a war?" she asked.

He nodded.

Still waters did run deep. "That was very brave of you."

"Yeah." He rolled his eyes. "Brave were the firefighters who ran up those stairs to try to get people out of the second tower before it fell. Brave were the people helping the victims on the ground instead of worrying about themselves. You wanna know what I did?"

"What?" she asked, unable to even imagine what it was like for him to be there that day. She had been away, traveling for business, and still had felt like a emotional zombie from just watching it on television from a thousand miles away.

"They'd already shut down the trains so I sprinted across the Brooklyn Bridge. Cell service was down so when I got to the other side I found a landline to use, called home and my mother drove down to get me." He looked disgusted with the memory.

"You were just a kid."

He shook his head. "Not that young. I was in boot camp with guys younger than me."

BB was obviously hardest on himself, but all she could think was that everything he'd done since—joining the Navy, then the SEALs, and now the special task force so secret her clearance allowed her to know it existed but not much else—more than made up for his perfectly normal actions on that horrible day.

He was modest, brave, gorgeous, sexy as hell—and too damn young for her to be thinking of him like that.

She quickly did the math. He'd said he'd started modeling in high school and had been on a shoot in Manhattan on September eleventh. He had to be what? About mid twenties now. And here she was hanging on to thirty-nine by the skin of her teeth.

Sure, she wasn't old enough to have birthed him, thank god for that, but she couldn't forget how he'd called her ma'am when they'd met.

He twisted in his seat to face her. "What about you?"

She raised a brow. "What *about* me?"

He smiled, the kind of smile that probably made women fall into his bed without a second thought. "Tell me about yourself. You don't wear a wedding ring, so I'm guessing you're not married."

He didn't pull any punches, did he? Was this payback for her prying into his past? She felt she had no other choice but to answer him.

"There's not much to tell. I'm divorced, no kids, no pets, not even a house plant. I've got an apartment in New York, a standing reservation at hotels in three states, and enough frequent flier miles to circumnavigate the globe. My job is my life. That's it." She shrugged.

He looked a little surprised at her brutally honest answer. But only for a moment, before he smiled again.

"So then you're available." He said it as a statement, not a question.

She laughed. "Why? You want to fix me up with your

father or something?"

"First of all, my mother would definitely object. But on top of that, a date with you would probably kill my father."

That could be the most intriguing compliment she'd ever received.

He continued with a confident smile, "So, where do you want to eat dinner tonight after we land?"

"Um, I was thinking the hotel restaurant, if that's okay."

"Sounds good." He grinned.

Why did it seem like their professional relationship had just taken a sharp left turn toward personal? And, dammit, why was her heart suddenly beating faster?

Katie considered that in the cab ride from the airport to the hotel where she checked herself and BB into a suite with two adjoining bedrooms. It had seemed like a good idea when she'd booked it, in case they needed to get work done in the room.

It seemed less so now as she glanced guiltily at the door separating them and wondered what BB was doing over there in his room.

The ringing of her cell phone saved her from picturing him in the shower.

She answered and pressed the phone to her ear. "Katie Jorgenson."

"Hey. It's me." Her assistant's voice came through the line.

Katie had been so flustered she'd forgotten to look at the caller ID. She hadn't been around BB for even a full day yet and she was behaving like an adolescent.

"Hi, Emily. I was about to call you." *Yeah, sure she was.*

"So? Tell me. Is he as gorgeous in person as he is in those pictures you showed me? Or is he a stuck-up asshole? Does he wear dog tags? Ooo, is he wearing camouflage?"

Katie laughed. "Yes, no, I don't know and lastly, no."

There was a brief pause as her overly energetic assistant digested her answers. "Wait, I confused myself. Tell me again."

Emily was loyal and organized, but she was also twenty-three with far too much *joie de vie*. Sometimes just speaking with her made Katie tired.

She stifled a sigh and went over the answers again. "He's absolutely perfect for the campaign. He's very good looking and not at all an asshole, as you put it so eloquently. No camouflage. He wore jeans and a T-shirt on the plane and the flight attendants, both male and female, were all drooling over him. And I don't know if he's wearing dog tags or not. I haven't seen him without his shirt yet."

"Yet? Woo hoo!" Emily whooped. "You go for it."

Katie shook her head but couldn't help but smile. "*I mean* we have the photo shoot tomorrow."

"Oh. Too bad. I got excited there for you for a minute. I thought you were making your move. I did book you that suite."

As if she needed reminding.

"Well, don't get excited. He's way too young for me." Katie considered that Emily, as painfully young as she seemed, was much more BB's dating demographic than herself. Talk about painful.

"What are you talking about? All the Hollywood actresses are dating, even marrying, younger guys. It's the norm now."

"Yeah, well, actresses can do it. I'm a marketing exec, not some star in Hollywood. My boobs are real and they sag and my face has never seen Botox and it shows. And, to add insult to injury, I think I need reading glasses."

She pictured herself, granny glasses dangling from a chain around her neck, and dating a man in his twenties. Nope. Not gonna happen.

"You're crazy. You look great and you know it. And it's been way too long since your last date. Promise me you're not going to close yourself off to the idea of letting something develop with him."

Katie didn't like the role reversal as her assistant lectured her.

"Promise . . ." Emily prompted when Katie didn't answer.

She closed her eyes. Sometimes it was just easier to give in. "Promise."

Taking a deep breath, she pictured the hoards of beautiful young women who would be drooling over him after the ad campaign hit. She might as well go stand on the tracks and wait for the next subway train. That would be just as stupid as falling for BB. It would probably hurt less too.

CHAPTER FIVE

"Relax." Suddenly Katie's voice was beside his ear.

He jumped, not because he was nervous about the photo shoot, but because he wasn't prepared for how the feel of her breath against his skin would cut right through him.

"I am relaxed." He took one step away from her and her sexy whispers, happy he'd put some distance between them so he couldn't smell her shampoo and picture her in the shower anymore.

Considering he was standing in nothing more than cotton briefs, it was no time to be reacting to her closeness.

They'd had dinner together the night before, and sat and talked much longer than they should have considering they had an early call for the shoot this morning. But he hadn't wanted to say goodnight.

Besides, no one could see if there were shadows under his eyes with all the makeup they'd slapped on him. And with the way they had him dressed—or rather undressed—nobody would be looking at his face anyway.

She laughed. "You don't look relaxed."

He sure couldn't tell her it wasn't the photo shoot that was making him nervous. He'd fallen right back into modeling like he'd never left it. It was that he'd had one hell of a dream about her just before waking this morning that had left him alone in bed with a raging hard-on. He'd thrown himself into the shower to deal with the physical aspect, but the mental anguish remained.

Of all mornings to have an underwear shoot. He backed away another pace.

"I'm really fine." He just needed to get far away from her. "Do you think I could maybe get a bottle of water?"

"Of course." She rushed across the room and he breathed a sigh of relief.

The feeling, however, was short lived. All too soon she was back.

He thought he was safe when the photographer started discussing the shot with her, until he heard Katie say, "I want to see hands on him."

"*Excusez-moi?*" the photographer asked, as confused as BB at that statement apparently.

"You've got great shots of him alone, Pierre. The dog tags against his bare chest." She glanced at him then back to the photographer. "And the camouflage pants open to show his abs and just the edge of the briefs. It's all great. But what if we got a few with a woman standing behind him while he's facing the camera? You don't see her except for her hands wrapping around him and kind of . . . groping."

Groping?

Pierre nodded. "*Oui*. Do it. Let me see how it looks."

The discussion became very hands-on and quick as a wink, Katie was pressed up behind him and groping.

The photographer grabbed his camera and started shooting.

BB set his jaw and tried to think of something else as Katie's manicured nail traced the line of hair on his abdomen that led down to his—

"Good, BB. Perfect! I love the facial expression. Mean and tough."

Great. BB was so glad Pierre was happy.

Meanwhile, since the studio was so hot because of all the lights, Katie had taken off her winter overcoat and suit jacket and was now down to just a sleeveless top. As she pressed close behind him, her flesh was pretty much adhered to his.

In fact, they'd been just like this, only reversed and naked, in his dream this morning.

"Katie. Slide just your fingertip under the elastic of the briefs," Pierre instructed.

The minute BB heard that, he knew he was in trouble. His mind went to bad, bad places and his body followed.

Katie slid her hand lower, her fingers slipping beneath the waistband of his underwear at the same time he felt his cock rise to the occasion.

He grabbed her hand, yanking it out of his briefs before taking a step away from her. As his face grew hot, he glanced at the photographer. "I'm sorry. I need a break."

Katie came around to stand in front of him. "What's wrong? Are you okay? Are the lights too hot?" Her eyes dropped for barely a second before she yanked her gaze up. As the color crept into her cheeks, she said, "Oh."

He was so appalled, that the situation in his briefs had pretty much remedied itself already. Even so, he'd never forget it. She was looking everywhere except at him when he said, "Katie, I'm sorry."

A little furrow appeared in-between Katie's brows when she finally made eye contact again. Even her frown was starting to look sexy to him. He was in sorry shape and all over one stupid dream.

"No, BB. *I'm* sorry. My hands were all over you. I didn't even ask if it was okay first."

Pierre threw his hands in he air. "He's sorry. She's sorry. *I'm* going to be sorry if I don't get these shots. He's a man. It happens. Get over it. We need to finish this today. The schedule you've set up is impossible. Transit ads in under twenty-four hours. I've never heard of such a thing. Come, Katie. Look and see if we've got something you can use so your soldier can change for the next shot."

With a final glance at BB, Katie followed the photographer to his computer.

Meanwhile, BB looked at the ice in the bin filled with water bottles across the room and considered if he could shove some cubes down his briefs instead of taking a cold shower.

The remainder of the day was filled with activity and people. BB was grateful for the distraction. It almost had him forgetting his humiliation. *Almost.*

He posed for some holiday shots where Pierre had him in nothing but red briefs with gold Christmas garland wrapped around his neck.

During that, Katie had stayed far away from him while he posed, keeping busy on her laptop while calling out suggestions of what the ad copy could read. Lines such as, *"Who will be in your stockings this holiday?"* and, *"Some packages just can't wait to be opened."*

Yup. Humiliating. All on top of his earlier public hard-on. He remembered very vividly why he'd quit this shit to crawl around in the mud instead.

And speaking of crawling in the mud . . . he posed for shots to be used strictly for the recruitment campaign too. He went from wearing a wet suit to camouflage pants, shirtless, smeared with greasepaint. Every shot was taken in front of a screen so the various backgrounds could be added later with a computer.

He changed more times than he could count but since he was grateful to be in clothes and not just underwear he wasn't complaining.

Katie spent most of her time choosing the shots to be used, working with the graphic designers on design and giving final approval to the proofs before sending them off to the printer.

Things moved fast. It was hard to believe the Milano holiday ad—the embarrassing underwear and garland shot—would be rush printed overnight and hanging in every subway car and even on the sides of a few buses by morning.

But even with as good as she was at her job he was more interested in her as a woman. He would have liked to have another evening with her alone, but instead they ate dinner with some execs from Andre Milano, corporate idiots with whom he had nothing in common.

As they all talked marketing and demographics, it gave BB a chance to observe Katie unnoticed. She was one hundred and ten percent devoted to her job, just as he was to his—his real job not this modeling gig. He could respect her dedication. Even as he wished he could make her forget everything about work and cut loose for a bit—with him.

Even now, back in the suite and looking exhausted but pretending she wasn't, Katie was still all business, briefing him for the interviews the next morning.

The last thing he wanted to do was talk about work, but she looked too tired to do what else he had in mind. And he definitely wanted her as an active participant if and when *that* happened.

"Katie?"

"Yeah?" She finally glanced up from her paper.

"It's late. Let's you and I go to bed." As a smile tickled his lips as he let the suggestive sentence hang in the air, just to see how she reacted. Apparently, he'd gotten over today's hard-on humiliation just fine.

She raised a brow and hesitated. Unfortunately, it looked as if her business-half won out over her feminine-half. She held up the list of questions. "We won't have time to go over this in the morning."

He pushed her hand and the paper down. "It'll be fine. I'll be up early."

A frown furrowed her brow. "But you have to be at *The Today Show* by seven for makeup, then over to *Live with Regis and Kelly* before nine. And then to *The View* for an eleven o'clock airing."

"Katie, I'm usually awake by five. Give me your questions and I'll go over them on my own. We can review them together while I'm in the makeup chair tomorrow morning, if you want."

He was sure the guys on the team would just love to mock

him for talking about makeup. Hopefully, they'd never find out.

"You're okay with that? You're not nervous about the interviews?"

He was, actually. Modeling was one thing, but live television was quite another.

Besides that, he was concerned about what he should and shouldn't say. He'd spent his entire career with the SEALs and the task force avoiding telling people what he did. Now he was supposed to get up and talk about special operations without spilling any state secrets.

On top of it all, he had to remember to plug their sponsor, Andre Milano. Considering all that, this was probably going to be his most difficult assignment to date, and that was saying something.

He should go over the questions a few times. In fact, they should probably practice. Have her interview him or something. But Katie looked ready to drop so he said, "I'm not worried and you shouldn't be either. Go to bed, Katie."

He grasped her by the elbows, about to spin her toward her door when he noticed the heat that blazed in her eyes when he touched her.

It disappeared as quickly as it had come, but *damn*, the fact it had been there at all made him think she might actually say yes if he did ask her to join him in his bed. Or in her bed. He wasn't picky.

CHAPTER SIX

BB was amazing.

Katie stood off-stage and watched with awe and something else that felt an awful lot like lust.

She'd been a little worried. After all, he was a model. It was the rare specimen of that breed who could carry on witty banter and field questions thrown at them by morning talk show hosts.

But BB had held his own with *The Today Show* team. Even though she could tell he had been a bit nervous that morning, he'd gotten quickly over it.

He was a natural.

And now on the set of *Live with Regis and Kelly*, Katie watched as BB stripped off his shirt at Kelly Ripa's request and dropped down for a push-up contest against Regis Philbin.

The crowd cheered wildly while Kelly counted the repetitions. The audience loved it. Hell, even the producer Michael Gelman loved it. They'd be replaying clips of this on every ABC affiliate all day long. Katie was sure of it.

She laughed as Kelly sat on BB's back to even the odds, and he good-naturedly accepted the handicap and still went on to win the contest. He complimented Regis on giving him a run for his money, presented him with a gift package of

Andre Milano briefs and the segment was over.

The station cut to a commercial and BB was back beside her, pulling his US Navy long-sleeved shirt back over his head. "So? How do you think it went? Was that okay?"

He really had to ask?

"Are you crazy? That was great. *You* were great."

More than happy with how things were turning out, Katie apparently lost her mind. Before she could stop herself, she threw her arms around his neck.

BB wrapped his arms around her waist. "Really? You think so?"

She swallowed hard at the contact. "Yeah, really."

"Thanks." Smiling, he leaned in.

Katie watched as his mouth got closer. He hovered near her lips, watching her. His arms around her tightened just a bit.

She drew in a breath. She couldn't do it. She couldn't close that small gap between them. She didn't have the guts.

Her insecurities overcame her. She was too old. He was too young. He worked for not one but two of her biggest clients. They had a professional relationship that would be jeopardized if they crossed this line.

Every thought must have shown on her face. He closed the distance, but it was to just brush a quick, chaste kiss across her cheek before he dropped his hands from her and moved away.

"On to the next show?" he asked as if nothing had happened.

As her heart thundered, she managed a nod. "Yeah."

CHAPTER SEVEN

A one-hour talk show later and they'd checked out of the hotel, picked up the rental car and started the two-hour drive north to BB's hometown.

BB was behind the wheel half listening to the Christmas carol being played on the radio as Katie read something on her computer while speaking on her cell phone. He was once again glad that the tools of his trade were more of the guns and ammo variety. This woman couldn't get away from work, or her assistant's phone calls, day or night.

He glanced at the winter-brown scenery around him. He hadn't been home for nearly a year. It had been too long and he was looking forward to his holiday leave, even if he did have more work to do on this assignment before he could get to the leave part.

"So here's the plan . . ."

Seeing she was off the phone and speaking to him now, he brought his attention back to Katie and said, "Okay. Shoot."

"We've got an interview with a local radio station broadcasting live from the Poughkeepsie Galleria Mall tomorrow."

Great. Nothing like the mall on a Saturday the week before Christmas.

"Time?" he asked.

"Six for the morning drive-time." She cringed.

BB guessed why and smiled. "Not a morning person?"

"Not exactly. I mean there's morning, and then there's *morning*. I prefer my workday to start about eight. Seven the earliest."

"That early, we'll miss the crowds, at least." That was worth the early hour in his opinion.

"There is that." She sighed. "Anyway, after that we have a photographer and reporter from the local newspaper meeting us at the Armed Forces Recruiting Center in Poughkeepsie where they'll take a few shots of you with the guys there."

He nodded, knowing exactly which recruiting center she was talking about. It was where he'd enlisted all those years ago. Moving past the nostalgia, he asked, "And what about tonight?"

"You actually have a night off. Drop me at the hotel and you can take the rental car. Just don't forget to get me tomorrow early enough to get to the mall by six."

"I'll get you at five-thirty."

She groaned. "It's still going to be dark that early."

"Yup." He smiled again at her expression, all while planning on how best to use his night off. If all went well, his night would involve Katie.

"I think the last time I saw five-thirty, it was because I'd never gotten to sleep the night before."

"Now that's a story I'd like to hear."

She laughed at his comment. "No, you wouldn't. I'd pulled an all-nighter for work. Believe me, my life's not that interesting."

"Yes, it is. And you are."

Katie met his gaze but then rolled her eyes. "Yeah, sure."

She really had no idea how fascinating she was. He'd have to show her.

"I want you to come and meet my family tonight. Come over for dinner."

Her eyes widened before she shook her head. "I couldn't do that."

"Why not?" he asked.

"I don't want to intrude."

"You're not intruding. I invited you."

"But your mom isn't expecting me . . ."

He laughed. "She has nine kids, plus all of our friends who are always stopping by. She cooks like there's an army coming for dinner every night."

She hesitated. "Are you sure?"

He nodded. "I'm sure. We'll get you checked into the hotel then head over."

Finally, she said, "Okay."

BB smiled as the sign for his exit came into view. "Good."

The trip from the hotel to his parents' house turned out to be quite an eye opener for BB.

He nearly put them both through the windshield when he saw, just in the nick of time, the red light. An actual traffic light was on his parents' street. What the hell was that about?

Down the way a bit, he realized why there was a sudden need for a traffic light on a road that had never had or needed one. The old farmer who used to supply the local horse owners with hay had finally sold out. There were now about two hundred brand new houses dotting what used to be farm land.

BB was all for progress, but he didn't like change. Not change like that anyway. He pulled the car into his parents' driveway, glad to see that at least his old house still looked the same. It was a relief, since it seemed everything else in his hometown had changed, right down to the addition of a Starbucks.

He was also happy when his mother, looking exactly the same as he remembered her, came out to greet him. After cutting the engine, he swung the car door open, stepped out and hugged her hard.

"I'm so happy you're home." There were tears in her eyes.

"I'm happy to be home." He turned to introduce Katie, and realized she was hanging back by the car, looking uncomfortable. Reaching out, he grabbed her hand and pulled her closer. "Mom, this is Katie."

He was about to explain who Katie was when his mother stepped forward and threw her arms around her, capturing her in a hug that had Katie's eyes widening.

"Oh my God. Billy Bob hasn't brought a girl home with him in years. It's so nice to meet you, Katie. Come inside and tell me how you two met, since it seems Billy Bob isn't going to." His mother shot him a frown.

BB stood and watched Katie, looking like a deer in headlights, get pulled into the house by his mother. Katie glanced back at him, no doubt looking for rescue. All he did was grin.

He could correct his mother's assumption, tell her they were colleagues, not dating, but he decided to wait a little while and see how things played out.

His personal appearances were almost over, for now anyway, and Katie was scheduled to leave after the interview tomorrow.

So far BB had managed to keep their relationship professional, mostly. But now that things were wrapping up, he wasn't going to let her hide behind her job any longer.

He might get shot down. Then again he might not. Just the thought of that had him smiling as he followed the two women into the house.

CHAPTER EIGHT

Katie sat in the rental car and looked sideways at BB as he drove to the hotel. It was the first time she had with him alone since arriving at his parents' house.

It had been quite an evening.

He noticed her looking at him. "What?"

She screwed up her face. "As if you don't know. You let your mother believe we're dating."

And no matter how many times Katie had explained to her, to them all, what her role was, they still believed she was his girlfriend and was just telling them how they'd met.

What had really gotten her thinking was that no one—not his parents, not his two brothers or his one sister who'd come for dinner—looked at all surprised at the idea of her and BB being together.

She'd gone to his home thinking she would be closer to his mother's age than his, but she'd been wrong.

Bogged down by her insecurities about his age—and hers—she really hadn't thought it through. She'd been foolish. BB was the youngest of nine. Of course his mother had to be much older than her. Even if she had started at eighteen and had one child every year for nine years, which wasn't likely, that would make her well into her fifties.

As it turned out, BB's mom was a warm, funny, but tough

as nails woman of about sixty. She was the kind who made everyone feel like family in her home.

The large old farmhouse, all decked out in lights and garlands for the holidays, was as welcoming as the family itself.

The house even smelled like Christmas, all pine and cinnamon. It had been too nice of a taste of what being a part of that family—of any family—would be like.

She looked over and saw BB smiling at her. "Maybe I didn't correct my family for a reason."

"And what reason would that be?" she asked.

He didn't answer as he concentrated on pulling across the on-coming traffic and into the hotel parking lot. It was the kind of hotel where each room had an entrance from the exterior, so BB parked the car in front of her room and cut the ignition.

"Because nothing would make me happier than if it were true." He got out, walked around and opened her door just as she was trying to digest that.

When she stood, he put a hand on each of her shoulders, and then moved to stroke her cheek with one thumb.

Her surprise at that was only surpassed when he bent his head and whispered, "I'm going to kiss you. If you don't want me to, you better say so quick."

Her brain had a lot to say, but none of it got out of her mouth before BB covered her lips with his.

His kiss was warm and soft and her knees nearly buckled from the sheer pleasure of it.

When his tongue found hers, a small sound escaped her throat.

He echoed it with a groan of his own before breaking away. "Let's go inside."

They were still standing in front of the open door of the car in the well-lit parking lot of the hotel. If they went inside, she knew exactly what would happen.

He noticed her hesitation. "What's wrong? Is it because you're my handler?"

Oh, she wanted to *handle* him all right. She controlled her adolescent giggle at that ridiculous thought and said, "Yes. Partly." But not mostly.

If she slept with him tonight, it would absolutely kill her when she saw him out in public with some young thing on his arm. And that's exactly what would happen.

How could it not? He was young and hot and a veritable chick magnet.

"Exactly how old are you, BB?"

"So that's it. The age thing." He held her face in two large hands and forced her to look into his eyes. "I have no problem that you're a few years older than me. In fact, I think that's one of the things that attracted me to you in the first place."

He moved to nuzzle her neck, his breath warm against her ear making it hard to talk, or even think. He was making it very difficult to resist him as he nibbled on her earlobe.

"You know," he continued. "There's nothing's sexier than a strong, confident, mature woman who knows her mind."

Mature. Poor choice on his part. The word knocked her out of her mute state. "You didn't answer the question. How old are you, BB?"

"I'm almost twenty-nine."

She laughed and pulled back. Only a man would try to make himself older. "So you're twenty-eight."

He rolled his eyes. "My birthday is in January, so I'm less than a month away from being twenty-nine. So what? How old are you?"

She employed his trick just to show him how impossible this situation was. "I'll be forty next birthday."

God, that sounded horrible coming out of her mouth. She hadn't thought she'd have problems with turning forty, until now.

"So you're thirty-nine. Eleven years. Big deal."

"It is a big deal."

BB pressed his lips together. "Katie, we're standing outside in the cold in the dark in a parking lot along Route 9.

Can we talk about this inside your room? Please?"

Dropping her gaze, she didn't answer. He was hard to resist but she had to.

He bent low and dipped his head to be able to see her as she looked away. "Why can't I come in?"

She sighed. "Because if you come in, you know what's going to happen."

He smiled and pulled her against him. "I know what I hope is going to happen."

She felt his arousal as he pressed against her. There was no doubt that he wanted her, in spite of the ridiculous difference in their ages.

Her heart pounded as she started to tremble. She swallowed hard, wondering if just giving in to this attraction would be the craziest thing she'd ever done, or just the most stupid. "Will you be able to still work with me in a professional aspect if we do this?" She couldn't believe she was even considering doing this.

"Yes. Will you?" he asked.

No, her brain yelled. But her traitorous mouth said, "Yes."

"Good." Grinning, BB slammed the car door before he grabbed her hand and pulled her toward the room.

All the while Katie cursed her assistant for even putting the idea of BB into her head.

CHAPTER NINE

Katie was fighting her attraction to him. Fighting it tooth and nail. BB could see that. He also saw the moment when she gave in to it, and it was like unleashing a wild cat.

She'd handed him the key, and he'd barely flipped on the light and shut the door behind him when the look Katie gave him tugged all the way down to his core.

He threw the key on the dresser and pulled her to him. She stepped into his arms and pressed right up against him. There was no way she'd miss feeling his arousal between them.

When her eyes narrowed and her lips parted, it was all the invitation BB needed. He couldn't decide which to do first, kiss her or undress her. He tried to do both at the same time, until she was tangled in the sleeves of her coat and laughing.

He had to laugh at himself too. "Sorry. This is no way for me to impress you."

"You already impressed me days ago." A small smile tipped up the corner of her mouth. "Besides, no one's shown this much enthusiasm around me in a long time."

He shook his head. "I don't know why not. You're incredible."

Not that knowing he was the only man in her life didn't make him happy. It definitely did. And he had all night to

221

show her exactly how happy he was to be there.

Slowing things down, he started to peel off the many winter layers separating them, starting with the coat, then the suit jacket.

He decided now was the perfect time to satisfy another one of his fantasies and reached behind her head. He pulled out the elastic band that confined her hair. Thick, silky locks tumbled down her back.

BB ran his fingers through the soft tresses. Her eyes closed as he massaged her scalp.

He took a shaky breath at the vision before him and was lost. "I've been wanting to do that since the first time I saw you in the commander's office."

Opening her eyes, she met his gaze and slipped both hands beneath his shirt, running them up his bare chest. "And I've been trying not to think about how much I've wanted to do this since I met you in your commander's office."

Deciding they'd both waited too long already, BB divested them both of their clothing until he was down to nothing but his Andre Milano briefs and she was in just her bra and underwear.

He reached behind her back to find the hooks when she stopped him.

She frowned. "Leave it on. Please?"

He stroked the smooth skin of her back. "Okay."

She'd get comfortable around him eventually. Until then, he didn't care what the hell she was wearing, as long as they could get to that big bed. And since it was a big bed and a small room, he barely had to take one step backward before he fell back onto the mattress and she tumbled on top of him.

Katie straddled him, two thin layers of cotton undergarments the only thing between them.

She moved and his length rubbed between her thighs. The friction sent a shiver through him. He fought to keep his eyes open so he could watch her. Her hair fell in loose waves around her face as she looked down at him with heavily lidded eyes.

She sighed. "BB." Katie said it as if she doubted they should be doing this, even as her hands roamed his chest.

Hoping she wasn't going to change her mind, he settled his hands on her hips and held her tight against him.

Perhaps a little incentive might help.

The smallest movement of his hips had the bulge in his briefs grinding against her most sensitive spot. Her eyes closed as a little sound of pleasure escaped from her.

"We'll take it slow as you want."

She released a shaky breath tinged with a laugh. "No. I don't want slow."

"No?" He lifted one brow.

"No." She brought his hand up to her mouth and kissed the palm, before saying, "I want you to fuck me until neither one of us can walk."

His eyes widened in surprise, which was quickly replaced by his desire. "Not a problem."

He would be more than happy to accommodate her request.

~ * ~

Having sex with a younger man—not to mention a man in the absolute height of physical condition—was an experience, to say the least.

Katie was too anxious for the main event to spend much time in the way of foreplay.

Sometimes foreplay was overrated. Looking down at the gorgeous specimen beneath her, she decided this was definitely one of those times.

A condom appeared from somewhere, she didn't care from where, and his briefs disappeared. Her underwear did too but she wasn't giving up the support her underwire bra provided her D-cup-sized breasts. Not if she was going to be on top.

Luckily, he didn't seem too concerned about her leaving it on. Especially not as she lowered herself onto his length with a shudder.

Eyes closed, she rocked against him, enjoying every stroke as each breath came faster.

He reached between them, but she shook her head and moved his hand away. "I'm good. It's good," she gasped.

"But I wanna make you come."

"Don't worry. I will." She felt her orgasm already starting to build.

Pressing closer, she ground against him until she was shaking. Her muscles clenched around his length, gripping him tight. He sucked in air between his teeth and released a groan.

Seeing the pleasure in his expression pushed her over the edge. She came hard and loud, leaving her throat dry and her limbs so shaky, she collapsed against his chest even though she knew he wasn't done yet.

Luckily, he was in better physical condition than she. Wrapping his arms around her, he rolled them both over. He looped an arm under her knee and plunged into her as the aftershocks of her orgasm still pulsed within her.

The hard, fast motion had her crying out and breathless as he pushed her toward a second climax.

CHAPTER TEN

BB watched Katie beneath him. When he felt her muscles grip him he knew—or at least hoped—what was about to come again.

A small frown furrowed her brow as she squeezed her eyes shut. Her lips parted and she held him close against her as she shattered for the second time. He closed his own eyes and concentrated on the amazing sensation of her pulsing around him.

He held back for as long as he could, then thrust into her as he came himself.

Finally, when the relentless waves of pleasure had stolen his strength and his breath, not to mention all rational thought, he collapsed on top of her.

"Holy mother of god, Katie. That was the most amazing thing I've ever felt."

She let out a breathy laugh. "Yeah, it was."

After a few moments of recovery, he blew out a breath and managed to lift himself on one elbow so he could see her.

He'd been with women his own age, and younger, and it had never been like that. He didn't think it wise to raise the comparison. "You're incredible."

She rolled her eyes. "It's just sex, BB. It's not exactly a

skill."

The way she did it, it was, but he didn't argue. Instead, he said, "Can I ask you something personal?"

Katie lifted one brow. "Since you're still inside me, I think it's probably okay."

He laughed, pulled out of her and rolled on his side. "Why did you get divorced?"

She looked surprised but said, "We were both young and, I guess, didn't know what the other one wanted in life."

"What did you want?" he asked, suddenly wanting to know everything about this woman.

"A successful career, a nice home of our own."

"What did he want?"

"Me barefoot and pregnant and us living in the apartment in the basement of his parents' house in the Bronx." She lifted one shoulder. "Maybe we didn't even know what we really wanted ourselves back then. Who knows?"

"I see the difficulty. How young were you when you got married?"

"We were about your age."

He wasn't going to let her start regretting this because of her age hang-up. "But you see the difference is, I know what I want."

"Oh really? And what's that?"

"I've already got it. I'm where I want to be in my career. My military career, that is, not the other one I've been forced back into. And I've got you right where I want you to be. With me."

"For now," she said.

He frowned. "Meaning?"

"This is one night, BB, maybe two. Then you'll go back to your life and I'll go back to mine."

He shook his head. "It doesn't have to be like that. Why can't we make happen what my family already assumed to be true? We both work a lot but that doesn't mean we can't date. We totally could."

She laughed. "So I'd be what? Your long distance

girlfriend?"

"Yeah. Why not? You'll come see me. I'll visit you."

"What about the future, BB? What do you want ten years from now?"

He shrugged. "I try not to worry much about the future. In my line of work, you live every day as it comes and thank God for it."

She pressed her lips together. "Let me tell you what I think. One day you're going to want to marry, settle down and have kids. I'm almost forty, BB. In ten years, I'll be fifty. Which means I can't be that woman for you. And as much as I understand your live for the moment philosophy, I can't warm your bed until you leave me for a younger woman who can have your babies."

She looked away but not before he saw tears shining in her eyes.

He clenched his jaw. "That's not fair, Katie. I would never use you then dump you. I'm not interested in a younger woman. If that was what I wanted, don't you think I'd be with one right now? I'm not here with you because you were convenient. I'm with you because I respect you professionally, I care about you personally, and I absolutely crave you physically."

She didn't talk but he could see she was listening, even as the tears tipped over onto her cheeks.

"And as for kids," he continued. "I grew up with eight older brothers and sisters. Everything I owned was a worn out old hand-me-down. And now I have more nieces and nephews than I can keep track of, and even though I love them all, what makes you think I want kids? For your information, when I got recruited for Zeta I decided I probably wouldn't ever have a family of my own. And I'm fine with that."

Her tears fell freely as she finally looked at him. "I know you believe what you're saying now. But I also believe I'm right. You just don't know it yet."

He shook his head, his anger growing in spite of her tears,

or maybe because of them. "You're wrong. You know, I would have understood if you couldn't be with me because of the nature of my job or the distance. But not because you're assuming I'm going to trade you in for someone younger. If you really think that of me, then maybe you're right. We shouldn't be together."

Standing, he ditched the condom in the trashcan and searched the floor for his clothes. He dressed as quickly as he could while trying to ignore the tears streaming silently down her face.

Hand on the door knob, he remembered his assignment wasn't over yet. Glancing back, he said, "I'll pick you up at five-thirty."

CHAPTER ELEVEN

Katie held herself together—mostly—until the door closed behind him, then the sobs she'd been controlling broke free.

Thank God she'd held them in until he was gone . . . and he *was* gone.

She'd managed to push him away, faster than she'd imagined possible. But better now then later. It would only hurt worse then.

Her cell phone rang in her purse. She leapt from the bed, cursing herself for hoping it was BB. She couldn't hope. Having hope would only devastate her.

She saw Emily's name on the read out and answered on a sob. "Oh, Emily."

"Katie? What happened?"

"I took your advice and had sex with him and then he wanted me to be his girlfriend but he's only twenty-eight and I'm too old to be a twenty-eight year old's girlfriend. I'm almost forty and then I'll be fifty and he'll want to have kids and my eggs are probably all shriveled up already and he's going to leave me for a younger woman, I know it, so I told him that. He looked so mad and then he left."

She'd cried her way through the whole short but sordid tale.

No, it wasn't professional to lay this on her assistant, but what choice did she have? She worked so damn much, she didn't have any actual friends.

Besides, it was Emily's fault she'd even been crazy enough to consider being with BB in the first place.

"Katie, you do realize you don't want to be with him because you're too afraid of being hurt to commit to a relationship, right?"

"Yes." She hated when Emily was right.

"So call him right now and tell him that. He'll forgive you."

"You think so?" There was that damn hope again. Katie was torn between beating it back and grabbing onto it with both hands.

"Yes, and if he doesn't, you don't want him anyway."

Such sage words from one so young. She'd really have to stop being such an age-ist. Katie vowed that if BB would forgive her, she'd never make age-based generalizations again.

A knock on the door had her spinning toward the sound.

Holding her breath, she heard BB say, "Katie?"

Her heart pounded. "Oh my God. Emily, he's outside knocking."

"See. I told you he'd forgive you. What the hell are you doing? Put down the phone and go open the door."

"Okay, bye." She disconnected the call and scrambled off the bed.

Tossing the cell onto the mattress, she had to search for her underwear on the floor. When she found them she tugged them on, almost falling on her ass in the process.

In only bra and panties, she ran for the door, pausing when she realized how bad she must look at the moment.

Fuck it. It was a miracle he was even there. She wasn't going to make him wait. She only hoped he would still want her once he saw her at her worst. But as Emily had said, if he didn't, then she wouldn't want him anyway.

The cold night air felt good against her hot, tear-streaked face as she opened the door. Realizing she was too naked to be standing in the doorway in full view of the parking lot, she stepped back.

BB took no time coming inside and slamming the door behind him. He grabbed her face in his hands and leaned low. His gaze locked on hers, he said, "I'm sorry I got angry. And I'm sorry I left."

"It's okay."

"No, it's not, but that's for me to deal with on my own." He shook his head. "What matters now is us."

"Us?" She swallowed hard.

"Yes. I won't let you push me away because you're afraid of something that isn't going to happen." He said it with a determined conviction that brought renewed tears to her eyes.

"I don't want to push you away. And I don't want to be afraid anymore. Will you help me stop being afraid?"

He nodded. "Yeah. I can do that. Can you do something for me?"

"Yes. What?"

"Don't leave when you were going to. Stay and spend Christmas with me and my family."

Her heart clenched. "I can do that."

"Good." Leaning in, he kissed her in a way that told her she was his and she'd better get used to it. She decided that was fine with her.

ABOUT THE AUTHOR

A top 10 *New York Times* bestselling author, Cat Johnson writes the *USA Today* bestselling Hot SEALs series, as well as contemporary romance featuring sexy alpha heroes who often wear cowboy or combat boots. Known for her creative marketing, Cat has sponsored bull-riding cowboys, used bologna to promote her romance novels, and owns a collection of camouflage and cowboy boots for book signings. She writes both full length and shorter works.

For more visit CatJohnson.net
Join the mailing list at catjohnson.net/news

Made in the USA
Coppell, TX
20 July 2023

19411376R00142